By Eudora Welty

A CURTAIN OF GREEN AND OTHER STORIES
THE ROBBER BRIDEGROOM
THE WIDE NET AND OTHER STORIES
DELTA WEDDING
THE GOLDEN APPLES
THE PONDER HEART
THE BRIDE OF THE INNISFALLEN AND OTHER STORIES
THIRTEEN STORIES
LOSING BATTLES
ONE TIME, ONE PLACE
THE OPTIMIST'S DAUGHTER
THE EYE OF THE STORY
THE COLLECTED STORIES OF EUDORA WELTY
ONE WRITER'S BEGINNINGS

THE PONDER HEART

The Ponder Heart

by EUDORA WELTY

DRAWINGS BY JOE KRUSH

A Harvest / HBJ Book
Harcourt Brace Jovanovich, Publishers
San Diego   New York   London

For permission to reprint THE PONDER HEART, the author wishes to thank the editors of *The New Yorker*, where it first appeared.

The towns of Clay and Polk are fictitious, and their inhabitants and situations products of the author's imagination, not intended to portray real people or real situations.

Library of Congress Cataloging in Publication Data
Welty, Eudora, 1909–
    The ponder heart.
    "A Harvest/HBJ book."
    I. Title.
PS3545.E6P7   1985   813'.52   84-22486
ISBN 0-15-672915-6

Printed in the United States of America

F G H I J

TO
MARY LOUISE ASWELL,
WILLIAM AND EMILY MAXWELL

My Uncle Daniel's just like your uncle, if you've got one—only he has one weakness. He loves society and he gets carried away. If he hears our voices, he'll come right down those stairs, supper ready or no. When he sees you sitting in the lobby of the Beulah, he'll take the other end of the sofa and then move closer up to see what you've got to say for yourself; and then he's liable to give you a little hug and start trying to give you something. Don't do you any good to be bashful. He won't let you refuse. All he might do is forget tomorrow what he gave you today, and give it to you all over again. Sweetest disposition in the world. That's his big gray Stetson hanging on the rack right over your head—see what a large head size he wears?

Things I could think of without being asked that he's given away would be—a string of hams, a fine suit of clothes, a white-face heifer calf, two trips to Memphis, pair of fantail pigeons, fine Shetland pony (loves children), brooder and incubator, good nanny goat, bad billy, cypress cistern, field of white Dutch clover, two iron wheels and some laying pullets (they were together), cow pasture during drouth (he has everlasting springs), innumerable fresh eggs, a pick-up truck—even his own cemetery lot, but they wouldn't accept it. And I'm not counting this week. He's been a general favorite all these years.

Grandpa Ponder (in his grave now) might have any fine day waked up to find himself in too pretty a fix to get out of, but he had too much character. And besides, Edna Earle, I used to say to myself, if the worst does come to the worst, Grandpa *is* rich.

When I used to spot Grandpa's Studebaker out front, lighting from the country, and Grandpa heading up the walk, with no Uncle Daniel by his side, and his beard beginning to shake under his chin, and he had a beautiful beard, I'd yell back to the kitchen, "Ada! Be making Mr. Sam some good strong iced tea!" Grandpa was of the old school, and wanted people to measure up—everybody in general, and Uncle Daniel and me in particular. He and Grandma raised me, too. "Clear out, you all," I'd say to who all was in here. "Here comes Grandpa Ponder, and no telling what he has to tell me." I was his favorite grandchild, besides being the only one left alive or in calling distance.

"Now what, sir?" I'd say to Grandpa. "Sit down first, on that good old sofa—give me your stick, and here comes you some strong tea. What's the latest?"

He'd come to tell me the latest Uncle Daniel had given away. The incubator to the letter carrier—that would be a likely thing, and just as easy for Uncle Daniel as parting with the rosebud out of his coat. Not that Uncle Daniel ever got a *letter* in his life, out of that old slow poke postman.

"I only wish for your sake, Grandpa," I'd say sometimes, "you'd never told Uncle Daniel all you had."

He'd say, "Miss, I didn't. And further than that, one thing I'm never going to tell him about is money. And don't let me hear you tell him, Edna Earle."

"Who's the smart one of the family?" I'd say, and give him a little peck.

My papa was Grandpa's oldest child and Uncle Daniel was Grandpa's baby. They had him late—mighty late. They used to let him skate on the dining room table. So that put Uncle Daniel and me pretty close together—we liked-to caught up with each other. I did pass him in the seventh grade, and hated to do it, but I was liable to have passed anybody. People told me I ought to have been the *teacher*.

It's always taken a lot out of me, being smart. I say to people who only pass through here, "Now just a minute. Not so fast. Could *you* hope to account for twelve bedrooms, two bathrooms, two staircases, five porches, lobby, dining room, pantry and kitchen, every day of your life, and still be out here looking pretty when they come in? And two Negroes? And that plant?" Most people ask the name of that plant before they leave. All I can tell them is, Grandma called it Miss Ouida Sampson after the lady that wished it on her. When I was younger, I used to take a blue ribbon on it at the County Fair. Now I just leave it alone. It blooms now and then.

But oh, when the place used to be busy! And when Uncle Daniel would start on a spree of giving away —it comes in sprees—and I would be trying to hold Grandpa down and account for this whole hotel at the same time—and Court would fling open in session across the street and the town fill up, up, up— and Mr. Springer would sure as Fate throttle into town and want that first-floor room, there where the door's open, and count on me to go to the movie with him, tired traveling man—oh, it was Edna Earle this, and Edna Earle that, every minute of my day and time. This is like the grave compared

You're only here because your car broke down, and I'm afraid you're allowing a Bodkin to fix it.

And listen: if you read, you'll put your eyes out. Let's just talk.

You'd know it was Uncle Daniel the minute you saw him. He's unmistakable. He's big and well known. He has the Ponder head—large, of course, and well set, with short white hair over it thick and curly, growing down his forehead round like a little bib. He has Grandma's complexion. And big, forget-me-not blue eyes like mine, and puts on a sweet red bow tie every morning, and carries a large-size Stetson in his hand—always just swept it off to somebody. He dresses fit to kill, you know, in a snow-white suit. But do you know he's up in his fifties now? Don't believe it if you don't want to. And still the sweetest, most unspoiled thing in the world. He has the nicest, politest manners—he's good as gold. And it's not just because he's kin to me I say it. I don't run the Beulah Hotel for nothing: I size people up: I'm sizing you up right now. People come here, pass through this book, in and out, over the years—and in the whole shooting-match, I don't care from where or how far they've come, not one can hold a candle to Uncle Daniel for looks or manners. If he ever did a thing to be sorry for, it's more than he ever intended.

Oh, even the children have always reckoned he

was theirs to play with. When they'd see him coming they'd start jumping up and down till he'd catch them and tickle their ribs and give them the change he carried. Grandpa used to make short work of them.

Grandpa worshiped Uncle Daniel. Oh, Grandpa in his panama and his seersucker suit, and Uncle Daniel in his red tie and Stetson and little Sweetheart rose in his lapel! They did set up a pair. Grandpa despised to come to town, but Uncle Daniel loved it, so Grandpa came in with him every Saturday. That was the way you knew where you were and the day of the week it was—those two hats announcing themselves, rounding the square and making it through the crowd. Uncle Daniel would always go a step or two behind, to exchange a few words, and Grandpa would go fording a way in front with his walking cane, through farmers and children and Negroes and dogs and the countryside in general. His nature was impatient, as time went by.

Nothing on earth, though, would have made Grandpa even consider getting strict with Uncle Daniel but Uncle Daniel giving away this hotel, of all things. He gave it to me, fifteen long years ago, and I don't know what it would have done without me. But "Edna Earle," says Grandpa, "this puts me in a quandary."

Not that Grandpa minded me having the hotel. It was Grandma's by inheritance, and used to be perfectly beautiful before it lost its paint, and the sign and the trees blew down in front, but he didn't care for where it stood, right in the heart of Clay. And with the town gone down so—with nearly all of *us* gone (Papa for one left home at an early age, nobody ever makes the mistake of asking about *him*, and Mama never did hold up—she just had me and quit; she was the last of the Bells)—and with the wrong element going spang through the middle of it at ninety miles an hour on that new highway, he'd a heap rather *not* have a hotel than have it. And it's true that often the people that come in off the road and demand a room right this minute, or ask you ahead what you have for dinner, are not the people you'd care to spend the rest of your life with at all. For Grandpa that settled it. He let Miss Cora Ewbanks run it as she pleased, and she was the one let the sign blow down, and all the rest. She died very shortly after she left it—an old maid.

The majority of what Uncle Daniel had given away up to then was stuff you could pick up and cart away—miscellaneous is a good word for it. But the Beulah was solid. It looked like it had dawned on Uncle Daniel about *property*. (Pastures don't count—you can take them back by just setting their cows back on the road.) Grandpa was getting plenty old, and he had a funny feeling that once *property* started going, next might go the Ponder place itself, and the land and the crop around it, and everything right out from under Uncle Daniel's feet, for all *you* could predict, once Grandpa wasn't there to stop him. Once Grandpa was in his grave, and Uncle Daniel shook free, he might succeed in giving those away to somebody not kin or responsible at all, or not even local, who might not understand what they had to do. Grandpa said that people exist in the realm of reason that are ready to take advantage of an open disposition, and the bank might be compelled to honor that—because of signatures or witnesses or whatever monkey-foolishness people go through with if they're strangers or up to something.

Grandpa just wanted to teach Uncle Daniel a lesson. But what he did was threaten him with the asylum. That wasn't the way to do it.

I said, "Grandpa, you're burning your bridges before you get to them, I think."

But Grandpa said, "Miss, I don't want to hear any more about it. I've warned him, now." So he warned him for nine years.

And as for Uncle Daniel, he went right ahead, attracting love and friendship with the best will and the lightest heart in the world. He loved being happy! He loved happiness like I love tea.

✦

And then in April, just at Easter time, Grandpa spent some money himself, got that new Studebaker, and without saying kiss-my-foot to me, Grandpa and old Judge Tip Clanahan up and took Uncle Daniel through the country to Jackson in that brand-new automobile, and consigned him.

"That'll correct him, I expect," said Grandpa.

Child-foolishness! Oh, Grandpa lived to be sorry. Imagine that house without Uncle Daniel in it. I grew up there, but all you really need to know about is it's a good three miles out in the country from where you are now, in woods full of hoot-owls.

To be fair, that wasn't till after Grandpa'd tried praying over Uncle Daniel for years and years, and worn out two preachers praying over them both. Only I was praying against Grandpa and preachers and Judge Tip Clanahan to boot, because whatever *you* say about it, I abhor the asylum.

Oh, of course, from the word Go, Uncle Daniel got more vacations than anybody else down there. In the first place, they couldn't find anything the matter with him, and in the second place, he was so precious that he only had to ask for something. It seemed to me he was back home visiting more than he ever was gone between times, and pop full of stories. He had a pass from the asylum, and my great-grandfather Bell had been a big railroad man, so he had a pass on the branch-line train, and it was the last year we had a passenger train at all, so it worked out grand. Little train just hauls cross-ties now. Everybody missed Uncle Daniel so bad while he was gone, they spent all their time at the post office sending him things to eat. Divinity travels perfectly, if you ever need to know.

Of course, let him come home and he'd give away something. You can't stop that all at once. He came home and gave the girl at the bank a trip to Lookout Mountain and Rock City Cave, and then was going along with her to watch her enjoy both, and who prevailed on him then? Edna Earle. I said, "Dear heart, *I* know the asylum's no place for you, but neither is the top of a real high mountain or a cave in the cold dark ground. Here's the place." And he said, "All right, Edna Earle, but make me some candy." He's good as gold, but you have to know the way to treat him; he's a man, the same as they all are.

But he had a heap to tell. You ought to have heard some of the tales! It didn't matter if you didn't know the people: something goes on there all the time! I hope I'm not speaking of kin of present company. We'd start laughing clear around town, the minute Uncle Daniel hopped off the train, and never let up till Grandpa came chugging in to get him, to set him on the down-train. Grandpa did keep at it. And I don't know how it worked, but Uncle Daniel *was* beginning to be less open-handed. He commenced slacking up on giving away with having so much to tell.

The sight of a stranger was always meat and drink to him. The stranger don't have to open his mouth. Uncle Daniel is ready to do all the talking. That's understood. I used to dread he might get hold of one of these occasional travelers that wouldn't come in unless they had to—the kind that would break in on a story with a set of questions, and wind it up with a list of what Uncle Daniel's faults were: some Yankee. But Uncle Daniel seemed to have a sixth sense and avoid those, and light on somebody from nearer home always. He'd be crazy about you.

Grandpa was a little inclined to slow him down, of course. He'd say, "Who?—What, Daniel?—When?—Start over!" He was the poorest listener in the world, though I ought not to say that now when he's in his grave. But all the time, whatever Uncle Daniel might take it into his head to tell you, rest assured it was the Lord's truth to start with, and exactly the way he'd see it. He never told a lie in his life. Grandpa couldn't get past that, poor Grandpa. That's why he never could punish him.

I used to say Mr. Springer was the perfect listener. A drug salesman with a wide, wide territory,

in seldom enough to forget between times, and knowing us well enough not to try to interrupt. And too
tired to object to hearing something over. If anything, he laughed too soon. He used to sit and beg
for Uncle Daniel's favorite tale, the one about the
time he turned the tables on Grandpa.

Turned the tables not on purpose! Uncle Daniel
is a perfect gentleman, and something like that has
to *happen;* he wouldn't contrive it.

Grandpa one time, for a treat, brought Uncle
Daniel home to vote, and took him back to the
asylum through the country, in the new Studebaker.
They started too early and got there too early—I
told them! And there was a new lady busying herself out at the front, instead of the good old one.
"Low-in-the-hole!" as Uncle Daniel says, the lady
asked *him* who the old *man* was. Uncle Daniel was
far and away the best dressed and most cheerful of
the two, of course. Uncle Daniel says, "Man alive!
Don't you know that's *Mr. Ponder?*" And the lady
was loading the Coca-Cola machine and says, "Oh,
foot, I can't remember everybody," and called somebody and they took Grandpa. Hat, stick, and everything, they backed him right down the hall and shut
the door on him boom. And Uncle Daniel waited
and dallied and had a Coca-Cola with his nickel
when they got cold, and then lifted his hat and po-

litely backed out the front door and found Grandpa's car with the engine running still under the crape
myrtle tree, and drove it on home and got here with
it—though by the time he did, he was as surprised
as Grandpa. And that's where he ends his story. Bless
his heart. And that's where Mr. Springer would turn
loose and laugh till Uncle Daniel had to beat him
on the back to save him.

The rest of it is, that down in Jackson, the madder
Grandpa got, the less stock they took in him, of
course. That's what crazy *is*. They took Grandpa's
walking stick away from him like he was anybody
else. Judge Tip Clanahan had to learn about it from
Uncle Daniel and then send down to get Grandpa
out, and when Grandpa did get loose, they nearly
gave him back the wrong stick. They would have
heard from him about *that*.

When Uncle Daniel got here with that tale,
everybody in town had a conniption fit trying to
believe it, except Judge Tip. Uncle Daniel thought
it was a joke on the *lady*. It took Grandpa all day
long from the time he left here to make it on back,
with the help of Judge Clanahan's long-legged
grandson and no telling what papers. *He* might as
well not have left home, he wouldn't stop to tell
us a word.

There's more than one moral to be drawn there,

as I told Mr. Springer at the time, about straying too far from where you're known and all—having too wide a territory. Especially if you light out wearing a seersucker suit you wouldn't let the rummage sale have, though it's old as the hills. By the time you have to *prove* who you are when you get there, it may be too late when you get back. *Think* about Grandpa Ponder having to call for witnesses the minute he gets fifty miles off in one direction. I think that helped put him in his grave. It went a long way toward making him touchy about what Uncle Daniel had gone and done in the meanwhile. You see, by the time Grandpa made it back, something had happened at home. Something will every time, if you're not there to see it.

Uncle Daniel had got clear up to his forties before we ever dreamed that such a thing as love flittered through his mind. He's so *sweet*. Sometimes I think if we hadn't showed him that widow! But he was bound to see her: he has eyes: Miss Teacake Magee, lived here all her life. She sings in the choir of the Baptist Church every blessed Sunday: couldn't get *her* out. And sings louder than all the rest put together, so loud it would make you lose your place.

I'll go back a little for a minute. Of course we're all good Presbyterians. Grandpa was an elder. The

Beulah Bible Class and the Beulah Hotel are both
named after Grandma. And my other grandma was
the second-to-longest-living Sunday School teacher
they've ever had, very highly regarded. My poor
little mama got a pageant written before she died,
and I still conduct the rummage sales for the Negroes every Saturday afternoon in the corner of the
yard and bring in a sum for the missionaries in Africa
that I think would surprise you.

Miss Teacake Magee is of course a Sistrunk (the
Sistrunks are *all* Baptists—big Baptists) and Professor Magee's widow. He wasn't professor *of* anything, just real smart—smarter than the Sistrunks,
anyway. He'd never worked either—he was like
Uncle Daniel in that respect. With Miss Teacake,
everything dates from "Since I lost Professor Magee." A passenger train hit him. That shows you
how long ago *his* time was.

Uncle Daniel *thought* what he was wild about at
that time was the Fair. And I kept saying to myself, maybe that *was* it. He carried my plant over
Monday, in the tub, and entered it for me as usual,
under "Best Other Than Named"—it took the blue
ribbon—and went on through the flowers and quilts
and the art, passing out compliments on both sides
of him, and out the other door of the Fine Arts
Tent and was loose on the midway. From then on,

the whole week long, he'd go back to the Fair every whipstitch—morning, noon, or night, hand in hand with any soul, man, woman, or child, that chose to let him—and spend his change on them and stay till the cows come home. He'd even go by himself. I went with him till I dropped. And we'd no more leave than he'd clamp my arm. "Edna Earle, look back yonder down the hill at all those lights still a-burning!" Like he'd never seen lights before. He'd say, "Sh! Listen at Intrepid Elsie Fleming!"

Intrepid Elsie Fleming rode a motorcycle around the Wall of Death—which let her do, if she wants to ride a motorcycle that bad. It was the time she wasn't riding I objected to—when she was out front on the platform warming up her motor. That was nearly the whole time. You could hear her day and night in the remotest parts of this hotel and with the sheet over your head, clear over the sound of the Merry-Go-Round and all. She dressed up in pants.

Uncle Daniel said he had to admire that. He admired everything he saw at the Fair that year, to tell the truth, and everything he heard, and always expected to win the Indian blanket; never did—*they* never let him. I'll never forget when I first realized what flittered through his mind.

He'd belted me into the Ferris Wheel, then van-

ished, instead of climbing into the next car. And the
first thing I made out from the middle of the air
was Uncle Daniel's big round hat up on the platform
of the Escapades side-show, right in the middle of
those ostrich plumes. There he was—passing down
the line of those girls doing their come-on dance out
front, and handing them out ice cream cones, right
while they were shaking their heels to the music, not
in very good time. He'd got the cream from the
Baptist ladies' tent—banana, and melting fast. And
I couldn't get off the Ferris Wheel till I'd been
around my nine times, no matter how often I told
them who I was. When I finally got loose, I flew
up to Uncle Daniel and he stood there and hardly
knew me, licking away and beside himself with pride
and joy. And his sixty cents was gone, too. Well,
he would have followed the Fair to Silver City when
it left, if I'd turned around good.

He kept telling me for a week after, that those
dancing girls wore beyond compare the prettiest
dresses and feather-pieces he ever saw on ladies'
backs in his life, and could dance like the fairies.
"They every one smiled at me," he said. "And yet
I liked Miss Elsie Fleming very well, too." So the
only thing to be thankful for is he didn't try to treat
Intrepid Elsie Fleming—she might have bitten him.

As for Grandpa, I didn't tell him about the twelve

banana ice cream cones and where they went, but he
heard—he played dominoes with Judge Tip—and as
soon as he got home from the Clanahans' he took a
spell with his heart. The Ponder heart! So of course
we were all running and flying to do his bidding,
everything under the sun he said. I never saw such
lovely things as people sent—I gained ten pounds,
and begged people to spare us more. Of course I
was running out there day and night and tending to
the Beulah between times. One morning when I
carried Grandpa his early coffee, which he wasn't
supposed to have, he said to me, "Edna Earle, I've
been debating, and I've just come to a conclusion."

"What now, Grandpa?" I said. "Tell me real
slow."

Well, he did, and to make a long story short, he
had his way; and after that he never had another
spell in his life till the one that killed him—when
Uncle Daniel had *his* way. The heart's a remarkable
thing, if you ask me. "I'm fixing to be strict for the
first time with the boy," was Grandpa's conclusion.
"I'm going to fork up a good wife for him. And
you put your mind on who."

"I'll do my best, Grandpa," I said. "But remember we haven't got the whole wide world to choose
from any more. Mamie Clanahan's already engaged
to the man that came to put the dial telephones in

Clay. Suppose we cross the street to the Baptist Church the first Sunday you're out of danger."

So up rose Miss Teacake Magee from the choir —her solo always came during collection, to cover up people rattling change and dropping money on the floor—and when I told Uncle Daniel to just listen to that, it didn't throw such a shadow over his countenance as you might have thought.

"Miss Teacake's got more breath in her than those at the Fair, that's what she's got," he whispers back to me. And before I could stop his hand, he'd dropped three silver dollars, his whole month's allowance, in the collection plate, with a clatter that echoed all over that church. Grandpa fished the dollars out when the plate came by him, and sent me a frown, but he didn't catch on. Uncle Daniel sat there with his mouth in an O clear through the rest of the solo. It seems to me it was "Work, for the Night Is Coming." But I was saying to myself, Well, Edna Earle, she's a Sistrunk. And a widow well taken care of. And she makes and sells those gorgeous cakes that melt in your mouth—she's an artist. Forget about her singing. So going out of church, I says, "Eureka, Grandpa. I've found her." And whispers in his ear.

"Go ahead, then, girl," says he.

If you'd ever known Grandpa, you'd have been

as surprised as I was when Grandpa didn't object right away, and conclude we'd better find somebody smarter than that or drop the whole idea. Grandpa would be a lot more willing to stalk up on a wedding and stop it, than to encourage one to go on. Anybody's—yours, mine, or the Queen of Sheba's. He regarded getting married as a show of weakness of character in nearly every case but his own, because he was smart enough to pick a wife very nearly as smart as he was. But he was ready to try anything once for Uncle Daniel, and Miss Teacake got by simply because Grandpa knew who she was—and a little bit because of her hair as black as tar—something she gets from Silver City and puts on herself in front of the mirror.

Poor Grandpa! Suppose I'd even *attempted*, over the years, to step off—I dread to think of the lengths Grandpa would have gone to to stop it. Of course, I'm intended to look after Uncle Daniel and everybody knows it, but in plenty of marriages there's three—three all your life. Because nearly everybody's got somebody. I used to think if I ever did step off with, say, Mr. Springer, Uncle Daniel wouldn't mind; he always could make Mr. Springer laugh. And I could name the oldest child after Grandpa and win him over quick before he knew it. Grandpa adored compliments, though he tried to hide it. Ponder Springer—that sounds perfectly plausible to me, or did at one time.

At any rate, Uncle Daniel and Miss Teacake got married. I just asked her for recipes enough times, and told her the real secret of cheese straws—beat it three hundred strokes—and took back a few unimportant things I've said about the Baptists. The wedding was at the Sistrunks', in the music room, and Miss Teacake insisted on singing at her own wedding—sang "The Sweetest Story Ever Told."

It was bad luck. The marriage didn't hold out. We were awfully disappointed in Miss Teacake, but glad to have Uncle Daniel back. What Uncle Daniel told me he didn't take to—I asked him because I was curious—was hearing spool-heels coming and going on Professor Magee's floor. But he never had a word to say against Miss Teacake: I think he liked her. Uncle Daniel has a remarkable affection for everybody and everything in creation. I asked him one question about her and got this hotel. Miss Teacake's settled down again now, and don't seem to be considering catching anybody else in particular. Still singing.

So Grandpa carried Uncle Daniel to the asylum, and before too long, Uncle Daniel turned the tables on Grandpa, and never had to go back *there*.

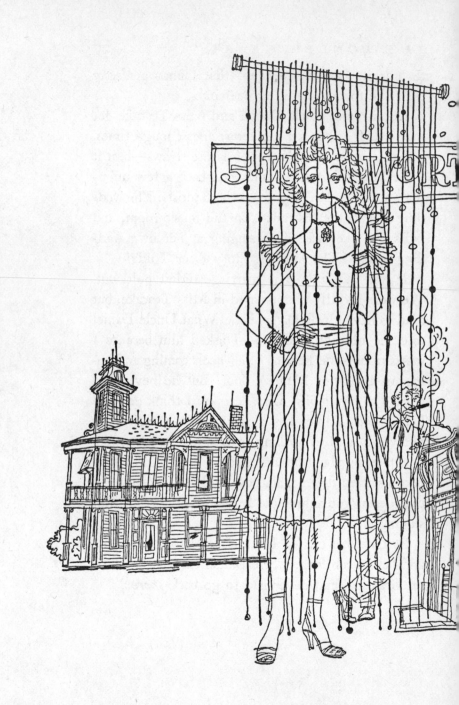

Meantime! Here traipsed into town a little thing
from away off down in the country. Near Polk: you
wouldn't have ever heard of Polk—I hadn't. Bonnie
Dee Peacock. A little thing with yellow, fluffy hair.

The Peacocks are the kind of people keep the
mirror outside on the front porch, and go out and
pick railroad lilies to bring inside the house, and wave
at trains till the day they die. The most they probably hoped for was that somebody'd come find oil
in the front yard and fly in the house and tell them
about it. Bonnie Dee was one of nine or ten, and no
bigger than a minute. A good gust of wind might
have carried her off any day.

She traipsed into Clay all by herself and lived and
boarded with some Bodkins on Depot Street. And

went to work in the ten cent store: all she knew how to do was make change.

So—that very day, after Uncle Daniel finished turning the tables and was just through telling us about it, and we were all having a conniption fit in here, Uncle Daniel moseyed down the street and in five minutes was inside the ten cent store. That was where he did all his shopping. He was intending to tell his story in there, I think, but instead of that, he was saying to the world in general and Bonnie Dee at the jewelry counter in particular, "I've got a great big house standing empty, and my father's Studebaker. Come on—marry me."

You see how things happen? Miss Lutie Powell, Uncle Daniel's old schoolteacher, was in there at the time buying a spool of thread, and she heard it— but just didn't believe it.

I was busy, busy, busy with two things that afternoon—worrying about what I'd say to Grandpa when he got back, and conducting my rummage sale in the yard. I might as well have been in Jericho. If Uncle Daniel had told me what he was going in the ten cent store to say—but I doubt strongly if he knew, himself, he's so sudden-quick—I could have pretty well predicted the answer. I could have predicted it partway. Because—Uncle Daniel can't help it!— he always makes everything sound grand. Home on the hilltop! Great big car! Negroes galore! Home-grown bacon and eggs and ham and fried grits and potato cakes and honey and molasses for breakfast every morning to start off with—you know, you don't have to have all the brilliance in the world to sound grand, or *be* grand either. It's a gift.

The first thing I knew of what transpired was two hours and a half later, when I was two dollars and ninety-five cents to the good of the heathen, selling away to the Negroes as hard as I could and dead on my feet in the yard. Then bang up against the hitching post at the curb pulls in that Studebaker. It honks, and the motor huffs and puffs, and the whole car's shaking all over like it does if you stop it too quick after running it too long. *It's* been go-ing all day, too. I shade my eyes and who do I see but old Narciss at the steering wheel. She's the cook out at the place. She's looking at me, very mournful and meaning and important. She always does look like that, but I never in my life knew she knew how to drive.

"Oh-oh," I says to the rummage sale. "Don't any-body touch a thing till I get back," and march out to meet it. There in the back seat sat Uncle Daniel big as life and right beside him Bonnie Dee Peacock, batting her eyes.

"Uncle Daniel, dear heart, why don't you get out

and come in?" I says, speaking just to him, first.

And Eva Sistrunk, the one that's a little older than me, just passing by with nothing to do, stopped in her tracks and politely listened in.

"Eva, how's your family?" says Uncle Daniel.

He was beaming away for all he was worth and shooting up his arm every minute to wave—of course Saturday traffic was traveling around the Square. Those people had just spent the morning waving him good-by, seeing him off to the asylum with Grandpa. By next time around they'd know everything. I look straight at Narciss.

Narciss is biding her time till she's got a big crowd and an outside ring of Negroes; then she sings out real high and sad, "Mr. Daniel done took a new wife, Miss Edna Earle."

You can't trust a one of them: a Negro we'd had her whole life long, older by far than I was, Grandma raised her from a child and brought her in out of the field to the kitchen and taught her everything she knew. Just because Uncle Daniel asked the favor, because the Studebaker wouldn't run for him the minute he got it back to where it belonged, Narciss hitched herself right in that front seat and up to the wheel and here they flew; got Bonnie Dee from in front of Woolworth's (and nobody saw it, which I think is worth mentioning—I believe they picked her up without stopping) and went kiting off to Silver City, and a justice of the peace with a sign in the yard married them. Uncle Daniel let Narciss pick out where to go, and Narciss picked out Silver City because she'd never been. None of them had ever been! It was the only spot in Creation they could have gone to without finding somebody that knew enough to call Clay 123 and I'd answer. Silver City's too progressive. Here they rolled back all three as pleased and proud as Punch at what they'd accomplished. It wasn't lost on me, for all the length Narciss had her mouth drawn down to.

I hadn't even had my bath! I just stood there, in my raggediest shade hat and that big black rummage sale purse weighting me down, all traffic stopped, and Eva Sistrunk with her face in mine just looking.

"So Miss Teacake's an old story," I said. "All right, Uncle Daniel—this makes you two."

"Makes me three," he says. "Hop out a minute, sugar, down in the road where Edna Earle and them can see you," he says to the child. But she sits there without a hat to her name, batting her eyes. "I married Mrs. Magee and I married this young lady, and way before that was the Tom Thumb Wedding— that was in *church*."

And it was. He has the memory of an elephant. When he was little he was in the Tom Thumb Wedding—Mama's pageant—and everybody said it was the sweetest miniature wedding that had ever been held here. He was the bridegroom and I believe to my soul Birdie Bodkin, the postmistress, was the bride—the Bodkins have gone down since. They left the platform together on an Irish Mail decorated with Southern Smilax, pumping hard. I've been told I was the flower girl, but I don't remember it—I don't remember it at all. And here Uncle Daniel sat, with that first little bride right on tap and *counting* her.

"Step out in the bright a minute, and see what I give you," he says to Bonnie Dee.

So she stood down in the road on one foot, dusty as could be, in a home-made pink voile dress that wouldn't have stood even a *short* trip. It was wrinkled as tissue paper.

And he says, "Look, Edna Earle. Look, you all. Couldn't you eat her up?"

I wish you could have seen Bonnie Dee! I wish you could. I guess I'd known she was living, but I'd never given her a real good look. She was just now getting her breath. Baby yellow hair, downy—like one of those dandelion puff-balls you can blow and tell the time by. And not a grain beneath. Now,

Uncle Daniel may not have a whole *lot* of brains, but what's there is Ponder, and no mistake about it. But poor little old Bonnie Dee! There's a world of difference. He talked and she just stood there and took her fill of my rummage sale, held up there under the tree, without offering a word. She was little and she was dainty, under the dust of that trip. But I could tell by her little coon eyes, she was shallow as they come.

"Turn around," I says as nicely as I can, "and let's see some more *of* you."

Nobody had to tell Bonnie Dee how to do that; she went puff-puff right on around, and gave a dip at the end.

Uncle Daniel hollers out to her, "That's my hotel, sugar." (He'd forgotten.) "Hop back in, and I'll show you my house."

I could have spanked her. She hopped in and he gave her a big kiss.

So Narciss pulls out the throttle, and don't back up but just cuts the corner through the crowd, and as they thunder off around the Courthouse she lets out real high and sad, "Miss Edna Earle, Mr. *Sam* ain't back yit, is he?" She was so proud of that ride she could die. She and Uncle Daniel rode off with what they had 'em—proud together.

Before I can turn around, Judge Tip Clanahan bawls down out of the window, "Edna Earle!" His office has been in the same place forever, next door up over the movie; but that never keeps me from jumping. "Now what? What am I going to do with Daniel, skin him? Or are you all going to kill him first? I tell you right here and now, I'm going to turn him over to DeYancey, if you don't mind out for him better than that."

Judge Tip gets us out of fixes.

"And hurt Uncle Daniel's feelings?" I calls up. DeYancey is just his grandson—young, and goes off on tangents.

"Come one thing more, I'll turn him over," Judge Tip bawls down to the street. "Where are we going to call the halt? Look where I'm having to send after Sam, none too sure to get him. I can't make a habit of that."

I left the whole array down there and climbed straight up those hot stairs and said to his face, "You ought to be ashamed, Judge Clanahan. I do mind out, everybody living minds out for Uncle Daniel, the best they can; it's you and Grandpa go too far with *discipline*. Just try to remember Uncle Daniel's blessed with a fond and loving heart, and two old domino cronies like you and Grandpa can't get around that by marrying him off to"—I made him a face like a Sistrunk—"and then unmarrying him, leaving him free for the next one, or running off with him to another place. That's child-foolishness, and I don't like to be fussed at in public at this time of the afternoon."

"Go on home, girl," says Judge Tip, "and get ready for your grandfather; he's loose and on his way. Already talked to DeYancey on the long-distance; don't know why he couldn't wait. I got no intention of washing my hands of Daniel or any other Ponder, and I'm not surprised for a minute at anything that transpires, only I'm a quiet studious man and don't take to all this commotion under my window." It woke him up, that's what.

"I don't see why there has to be any commotion anywhere," I says—and down on the street I made up my mind I'd say that to everybody. "People get married beneath them every day, and I don't see any sign of the world coming to an end. Don't be so small-town."

That held them, till Grandpa got back.

He got back sooner than I dreamed. I shook my big purse at him, when the car went by, to head him off, but he and DeYancey just hightailed it straight through town and out to the place. Nearly everybody still in the house along the way got out front in time to see them pass. I understand Miss Teacake Magee

even drove by Ponder Hill, pretending she was looking for wild plums. I said, Edna Earle, *you'd* better
get on out there.

All right, I said, but let me get *one* bath. It generally takes three, running this hotel on a summer
day. I said shoo to the rummage sale and let them
go on to the store.

While I was in the tub, ring went the telephone.
Mr. Springer got to town just in time to answer it.
I had to come down in front of him in my kimona,
and there was DeYancey, calling from the crossroads
store; I could hear their two good-for-nothing ca-
naries. I fussed at him for not stopping here with
Grandpa, because he might know I'd have something
to tell him.

DeYancey said *he* had a surprise for *me*, that he'd
better not tell me in front of a lot of people. I could
have sworn I heard Eva Sistrunk swallow.

"Tell me quick, DeYancey Clanahan," I says.
"I've all but got my hat on now—I *think* I know
what it is."

DeYancey only starts at the beginning. He said he
and Grandpa pulled up under the tree at the Ponder
place and went marching in by the front door. (I
told him they hadn't been beat home by much. Mr.
Springer called from his room that to Silver City and
back and to the asylum and back is just about equal

distance.) DeYancey said they heard running feet over their heads, and running feet on the stairs—and whisk through the old bead curtains of the parlor came somebody that poor Grandpa had never laid eyes on in his life or dreamed existed. "She'd been upstairs, downstairs, and in my lady's chamber," says DeYancey. "She was very much at home."

"No surprise so far," I says. "Bonnie Dee Peacock."

"All in pink," he said, like I wasn't telling him a bit. "And she'd picked one of Narciss's nasturtiums and had it in her mouth like a pipe, sucking the stem. She ran to the parlor windows and took a good look out of each one." He said Uncle Daniel came in behind her and after he kissed Grandpa, stepped to the mantel and rested his elbow on it in a kind of grand way. They smelled awful smoke—he had one of Grandpa's cigars lighted. Narciss was singing hallelujah somewhere off.

I said, "But DeYancey, you're leaving out what I want to hear—the words. What did Grandpa say?"

DeYancey said Grandpa *whispered*.

"I don't believe you."

DeYancey said, "It's all true. He whispered, and said 'They're right.' "

"Who?" I said.

"Well, the Clanahans," said DeYancey. "He whispered—" and DeYancey whispered, all hollow and full of birdsinging over the wires, with Lord knows who not with us—" 'When the brains were being handed around, my son Daniel was standing behind the door.' "

"Help," I said. "And did Uncle Daniel hear it? Let me go, DeYancey, I haven't got time for conversation. I've got to get out there and stand up for both of them."

"Don't you want to hear the surprise?" he says.

Well, he *did* have a surprise; he just had to get to it. Do you know it turned out that she'd just married Uncle Daniel *on trial?* Miss Bonnie Dee Peacock of Polk took a red nasturtium out of her mouth to say that was the best she could do.

After that, Grandpa just pounded with his stick and sent DeYancey out of his sight, with a message he would speak to me in the morning. And when he was getting his car out of the yard, DeYancey said, Narciss had the fattest chicken of all down on the block, and hollered at him, "We's goin' to keep her!" and brought her ax down whack.

"Just hang up and go home and take a bath, DeYancey," I says. "I've heard all I'm going to. I'm going to put on my hat."

Well, it's our hearts. We run to sudden ends, all we Ponders. I say it's our hearts, though Dr. Ewbanks declares Grandpa just popped a blood vessel.

Grandpa, Uncle Daniel, and Bonnie Dee still in pink were all about to sit down. I was just walking in the door—smelled chicken. Uncle Daniel says to me, "Just in time, Edna Earle. Poor Papa! You know, Edna Earle, he's hard to please."

And lo and behold.

We had the funeral in the Presbyterian Church, of course, and it was packed. I haven't been able to think of anybody that didn't come. It *had* mortified the Sistrunks that following behind one of them so close would come a Peacock; but with Grandpa going the sudden way he did, they rallied, and turned up in their best, and Miss Teacake asked to be allowed to sing. "Beautiful Isle of Somewhere" was her choice.

Uncle Daniel held every eye at the services. That was the best thing in the world for Uncle Daniel, because it distracted him from what was going on. Oh, he hates sickness and death, will hardly come in the room with it! He can't abide funerals. The reason every eye was on him was not just because he was rich as Croesus now, but he looked different. Bonnie Dee had started in on him and cut his hair.

Now I'll tell you about Bonnie Dee. Bonnie Dee could make change, and Bonnie Dee could cut hair.

If you ask me can I do either, the answer is no. Bonnie Dee may have been tongue-tied in public and hardly able to stand in high heels, till she learned how, but she could cut your hair to a fare-ye-well, to within a good inch of your life, if you put a pair of scissors in her hand. Uncle Daniel used to look like a senator. But that day his hair wasn't much longer than the fuzz of a peach. Uncle Daniel still keeps it like that—he loves himself that way.

Oh, but he was proud of her. "She's a natural-born barber," he said, "and pretty as a doll. What would I do without her?" He had the hardware salesman bring her a whole line of scissors and sharp blades. I was afraid she'd fringe everything in the house.

Well! Ignorance is bliss.

Except Bonnie Dee, poor little old thing, didn't know how to smile. *Yawned* all the time, like cats do. So delicate and dainty she didn't even have any heels to speak of—she didn't stick out anywhere, and I don't know why you couldn't see through her. Seventeen years old and seemed like she just stayed seventeen.

They had that grand Narciss—had her and never appreciated her. It didn't seem to me they ate out there near enough to keep her happy. It had turned out Narciss could sit at a wheel and drive, of course

—her and Grandpa's Studebaker both getting older by the minute, but she could still reach the pedals and they'd still catch, a little. Where they headed for, of course, was right here—a good safe place to end up, with the hitching post there to catch them at the foot of the walk. They sashayed in at the front —Narciss sashayed in at the back—and all ate with me.

That's how everybody—me and whoever was in here at the time, drummers, boarders, lawyers, and strangers—had to listen to Uncle Daniel mirate and gyrate over Bonnie Dee. With her right there at the table. We had to take on over her too, every last one of us, and tell him how pretty and smart we thought she was. It didn't bother her one whit. I don't think she was listening to amount to a row of pins. You couldn't tell. She just sat and picked at the Beulah food like a canary bird, and by the time Uncle Daniel was through eating and talking and pulled her up, it would be too late for the show for everybody. So he'd holler Narciss out of the back and they'd all three hop back in the car and go chugging home.

Now the only bad thing about the Ponder place is where it is. Poor Grandpa had picked him a good high spot to build the house on, where he could see all around him and if anybody was coming. And that

turned out to be miles from anywhere. He filled up
the house with rooms, rooms, rooms, and the rooms
with furniture, furniture, furniture, all before he let
Grandma in it. And then of course she brought her
own perfectly good rosewood in right on top of it.
And he'd trimmed the house inside and outside, top-
side and bottom, with every trimming he could get
his hands on or money could buy. And painted the
whole thing bright as a railroad station. Anything to
outdo the Beulah Hotel.

And I think maybe he did outdo it. For one thing
he sprinkled that roof with lightning rods the way
Grandma would sprinkle coconut on a cake, and was
just as pleased with himself as she was with herself.
Remarkable. I don't think it ever occurred to either
one of *them* that they lived far out: they were so
evenly matched. It took Grandpa years to catch on
it was lonesome. They considered *town* was far.

I've sometimes thought of turning that place *into*
something, if and when it ever comes down to me
and I can get the grass out of it. Nobody lives in the
house now. The Pepper family we've got on the
place don't do a thing but run it. A chinchilla farm
may be the answer. But that's the future. Don't think
about it, Edna Earle, I say. So I just cut out a little
ad about a booklet that you can send off for, and put
it away in a drawer—I forget where.

So the marriage trial—only it had completely left our minds it was one—went on for five years and six months, and Bonnie Dee, if you please, decided No.

Not that she said as much to a soul: she was tongue-tied when it came to words. She left a note written in a pencil tablet on the kitchen table, and when Narciss went out to cut up the chicken, she found it. She carried it to Uncle Daniel in the barn, and Uncle Daniel read it to her out loud. Then they both sat down on the floor and cried. It said, "Have left out. Good-by and good luck, your friend, Mrs. Bonnie Dee Peacock Ponder." We don't even know which one of them it was *to*.

Then she just traipsed out to the crossroads and

flagged down the north-bound bus with her little handkerchief—oh, she was seen. A dozen people must have been in the bushes and seen her, or known somebody that did, and they all came and told me about it. Though nobody at all appeared to tell me where she got off.

It's not beyond me. You see, poor, trusting Uncle Daniel carried that child out there and set her down in a big house with a lot of rooms and corners, with Negroes to wait on her, and she wasn't used to a bit of it. She wasn't used to keeping house at all except by fits and starts, much less telling Negroes what to do. And she didn't know what to do with herself all day. But how would she tell him a thing like that? He was older than she was, and he was good as gold, and he was prominent. And he wasn't even there all the time—*Uncle Daniel* couldn't stay home. He wanted her there, all right, waiting when he got back, but he made Narciss bring him in town first, every night, so he could have a little better audience. He wanted to tell about how happy he was.

The way I look back at Bonnie Dee, her story was this. She'd come up from the country—and before she knew it, she was right back in the country. Married or no. She was away out yonder on Ponder Hill and nothing to do and nothing to play with in sight but the Negroes' dogs and the Peppers' cats and one little frizzly hen. From the kind of long pink finger-nails she kept in the ten cent store, that hadn't been her idea at all. Not her dream.

I think they behaved. I don't think they fought all over the place, like the Clanahan girls and the Sistrunk boys when they marry. They wouldn't know how. Uncle Daniel never heard a cross word in his life. Even if Bonnie Dee, with her origins, could turn and spit like a cat, I hardly think she would around Uncle Daniel. That wouldn't be called for.

I don't blame Bonnie Dee, don't blame her for a minute. I could just beat her on the head, that's all.

And I did think one thing was the funniest joke on her in the world: Uncle Daniel didn't give her any money. Not a cent. I discovered that one day. I don't think it ever occurred to him, to give anything to Bonnie Dee. Because he *had* her. (When she said "trial," that didn't mean anything to Uncle Daniel that would alarm him. The only kind of trials he knew about were the ones across the street from the Beulah, in the Courthouse—he was fond of those.)

I passed her some money myself now and then— or I bought her something ladylike to put on her back. I couldn't just leave her the way she was! She never said more than "Thank you."

Of course, Uncle Daniel wasn't used to money,

himself. With Grandpa in his grave, it was Mr. Sis-trunk at the bank that gave him his allowance, three dollars a month, and he spent that mostly the first day, on children—they were the ones came out and asked him for things. Uncle Daniel was used to purely being rich, not having money. The riches were all off in the clouds somewhere—like true love is, I guess, like a castle in the sky, where he could just sit and dream about it being up there for him. But money wouldn't be safe with him a minute—it would be like giving matches to a child.

Well! How the whole town did feel it when Bon-nie Dee lit out!

When we sat in here night after night and saw that pearly gray Stetson coming in view, and moving up the walk, all we could do was hope and pray Uncle Daniel was here to tell us she was back. But she wasn't. He'd peep in both windows from the porch, then go around by the back and come in through the kitchen so he could speak to Ada. He'd point out what he'd have on his plate—usually ham and steak and chicken and cornbread and sweet potatoes and fried okra and tomatoes and onion-and-egg—plus ba-nana pie—and take his seat in the dining room and when it came go "Ughmmmmmmm!" One big groan.

And I'd call everybody to supper.

Uncle Daniel would greet us at the table. "Have

you seen her, son? Has a soul here seen my wife?
Man alive! My wife's done left me out there by
myself in the empty house! Oh, you'd know her if
you came across her—she's tiny as a fairy and pretty
as a doll. And smart beyond compare, boys." (That's
what she told him.) "And now she's gone, clean as
a whistle." There'd be a little crowd sitting close on
both sides before he knew it. And he'd go into his
tale.

It would be like drawing his eye-teeth not to let
him go on and tell it, though it was steadily breaking his heart. Like he used to be bound and deter-
mined to give you a present, but that was a habit
he'd outgrown and forgotten now. It was safer for
his welfare to let him talk than let him give away,
but harder on his constitution. On everybody's.

But I don't think he could bring himself to believe the story till he'd heard himself tell it again.
And every night, when he'd come to the end, he'd
screw his eyes up tight with fresh tears, and stand
up and kiss me good night and pull his hat down off
the rack. So I'd holler Narciss out of the kitchen for
him—she came out looking sadder and sadder every
time too—and she'd carry him on home. I knew he'd
be back the next night.

Eva Sistrunk said she couldn't make up her mind
whether it was good or bad for this hotel—though

I don't believe she was asked. Things would look like a birthday party inside, such a fine crowd—some out-of-town people hanging onto the story and commiserating with Uncle Daniel, and the Clay people cheering him on, clapping him on the shoulder. Everybody here, young or old, knew what to say as well as he did. When he sat there at the big middle table he always headed for, all dressed up in sparkling white and his red tie shining, with his plate heaped up to overflowing and his knife and fork in hand, ready and waiting to begin his tale of woe, he'd be in good view from the highway both north and south, and it was real prosperous-looking in here —till he came to the part about the note, of course, and how Narciss lightfooted it out to the barn and handed it to him so pleased, where he was feeding his calf—and he broke down at the table and ruined it all.

But that's what he came in here for—cry. And to eat in company. He ate me out of house and home, not so much to be eating as to be consoling himself and us (we begged him to eat, not cry), but some nights, when he had a full house, I had to flit along by the back of his chair and say under my breath, "Uncle Daniel! F. H. B.!"

He'd just catch me and say, "Edna Earle! Where do you suppose she could've got to by this time?

Memphis?" Memphis was about the limit Uncle
Daniel could stand to think of. That's where everybody else had it in mind she went, too. That's where
they'd go.

Somebody'd always be fool enough to ask Uncle
Daniel how come he didn't hop in his car and drive
on up to Memphis and look for Bonnie Dee, if he
wanted her back that bad. Some brand-new salesman
would have to say, "It can be driven in three hours
and forty-five minutes."

"Believe that's just what I'll do, sir!" Uncle
Daniel would say, to be nice. "Yes sir, I'll go up
there in the cool of the morning, and let you know
what I find, too." "Miss Elsie Fleming—I wonder
where *she* is," he said now and then, too. Well, he
just never can forget anybody.

But he wouldn't dream of going to Memphis, to
find Bonnie Dee or Intrepid Elsie Fleming or you
or anybody else. Uncle Daniel belongs in Clay, and
by now he's smart enough to know it; and if he
wasn't, I'd tell him.

"Never mind, Uncle Daniel," I'd come up again
and say when the tears fell. "Have a Fatima." He
adores to smoke those. I order off after them for
him, and always keep an extra supply on hand. And
I'd light him one.

I don't really think Uncle Daniel missed Bonnie Dee as much as he thought he did. He had me. He appeared at the Beulah every night of the world, sure as shooting, and every morning to boot, and of course when he came down sick out there, he hollered for Edna Earle.

I locked up the Beulah—well, it wouldn't lock, but I spoke to it and said "Burglars, stay away"— and went out to Ponder Hill in my trusty Ford to take care of him. When I got there, I missed Grandpa meeting me in the hall and telling me this had put him in a quandary.

The house is almost exactly the same size as the hotel, but it's a mile easier to run. If you know what you want done, you can just ask in the morning for how many Negroes you want that day, and Uncle Daniel hollers them in for you out of the fields, and they come just like for Grandpa. They don't know anything, but you can try telling them and see what happens. And there was always Narciss. By now she had a black smear across all her aprons, that the steering wheel made on her stomach; she sat up so close to the windshield to see how to drive. I made her get back to the stove.

I missed my city lights. I guess electricity was about the bane of Grandpa's life, next to weakness of character. Some power fellow was eternally coming

out there and wanting to string it up to the house,
and Grandpa'd say, "Young man, do you want to
draw the lightning out here to me when I've done
everything I know how to prevent it?" and throw
him out. We all grew up learning to fend for ourselves. Though *you* may not be able to read in the
dark, I can. But all the other children and grandchildren went away to the ends of the earth or died
and left only me and Uncle Daniel—the two favor-
ites. So we couldn't leave each other.

As a matter of fact, when I went back in that
house to look after Uncle Daniel when he was sick,
I'd have been lonesome myself if I hadn't liked to
read and had good eyes. I'm a great reader that never
has time to read.

Little old Bonnie Dee had six years of *True Love
Story* and six years of *Movie Mirror* stacked up on
the sewing machine in my room (she never hesitated
to shift the furniture) and the hatrack in the hall,
and down behind the pillows on the sofa. She must
have read her heart out. Or at least she'd cut all the
coupons out with her scissors. I saw by the holes she'd
left where she'd sent off for all kinds of things—you
know, wherever they showed the postman smiling in
the ad. I figured she must have got back, sometime
or other, twenty-four samples of world-famous per-
fumes; and a free booklet on how to speak and write

masterly English from a Mr. Cody who looks a great deal like Professor Magee from Clay, who's been dead for years; and a free piano lesson to prove you can amaze your friends; and a set of Balzac to examine ten days free of charge, but she must have decided against it—I looked everywhere. So there were holes in the stories all the way through, but they wouldn't have lasted me long anyway. I read *The House of a Thousand Candles* for the thousandth time; and the rest of the time I cleaned house. The hotter it is, the faster I go.

Uncle Daniel was happy no matter what I was doing. He wasn't really sick: I diagnosed him. Oh, he might have had a little malaria—he took his quinine when I gave it to him. Mainly, he just didn't want to be by himself. He wanted somebody closer than three miles away when he had something to say *right then*. There's something I think's better to have than love, and if you want me to, I'll tell you what it is—that's company. That's one reason Uncle Daniel enjoyed life even in Jackson—he was surrounded there.

"Why don't you come on into town, Uncle Daniel," I said, "and stay at the Beulah with me? I need to get the windows washed there too."

"No indeed," he says. "If she comes back, she'll come back here where she left off. Pretty thing, if she'd come in the door this minute, I'd eat her up."

But, "Oh, Edna Earle, where did she go?" That's what he began and ended his day with, that was the tail to all his stories. "Where has Bonnie Dee gone?" So after I'd heard that refrain enough times, I took myself into town and climbed the stairs to Judge Tip Clanahan's office. I caught him with his feet up on the wall, trying on fishing boots. I'm afraid De-Yancey was already fishing.

Well, as I opened the subject by saying when I sat down, I can't *help* being smarter than Uncle Daniel. I don't even try, myself, to make people happy the way they should be: they're so stubborn. I just try to give them what they think they want. Ask me to do you the most outlandish favor tomorrow, and I'll do it. Just don't come running to me afterwards and ask me how come.

So we compromised on a three-day ad in the Memphis *Commercial Appeal.* (Judge Tip wanted to let well enough alone.) Because it developed that Mr. Springer—my friend—had come through yesterday, and sailed right on to Silver City for the night; but had idled his engine long enough at the drugstore corner to call to DeYancey Clanahan, who was getting a haircut from Mr. Wesley Bodkin next door, to tell him *he* saw Bonnie Dee Peacock the day before in Memphis, when he was passing through. Saw

her in Woolworth's. She was trying to buy something. And had her sister with her. Mr. Springer told
DeYancey and Mr. Bodkin that he raised his hat and
tendered a remark to her, and she put out her tongue
at him. That was enough for Mr. Springer.

Looks like he would have come straight to me
with that, but he said he didn't know where I was.
Everybody else knew where I was. Everybody knows
where everybody is, if they really want to find them.
But I suppose if the door to the Beulah is ever pulled
to, and Ada's not out cutting the grass, Mr. Springer
will always assume that I'm dead.

Well, I mailed in the ad without saying a word
to the post office, and sat back with folded hands.
Judge Tip and I didn't breathe a word of what we'd
done. Uncle Daniel hopes too much as it is. And he'd
rather get a surprise than fly. Besides, it would have
hurt his feelings more than anything else I know of
to discover the entire world could pick up the morning paper and read at a glance what had happened
to him, without him being the one to tell it.

Lo and behold, they printed it. I put it in the
form of a poem while I was about it. It's called
"Come Back to Clay."

Bonnie Dee Ponder, come back to Clay.
Many are tired of you being away.

O listen to me, Bonnie Dee Ponder,
Come back to Clay, or husband will wonder.
Please to no more wander.
As of even date, all is forgiven.
Also, retroactive allowance will be given.
House from top to bottom now spick and span,
Come back to Clay the minute you can.
Signed, Edna Earle Ponder.
P.S. Do not try to write a letter,
Just come, the sooner the better.

Judge Tip horned in on two lines, and I don't think he helped it any. But it was better then than it may sound now. I cut it out and put it in a drawer to show my grandchildren.

I don't believe for a minute that she saw it. Somebody with bright eyes, who did, went and told her. And here she came. Nine forty-five the next morning, in she walked at the front door. She looked just exactly the same—seventeen.

The first I knew about it, Uncle Daniel hollered from the dining room out to me in the kitchen, "Edna Earle! Edna Earle! Make haste! She's fixing to cut my throat!"

I'd been up for hours. I was having Narciss put up his peaches. But I came when he called, spoon and all. He'd jumped up on top of the dining room table where he'd been having a little buttermilk and crackers after breakfast.

I said, "Why, climb down, Uncle Daniel, it's only Bonnie Dee. I thought that was what you wanted! You'll spill your milk."

"Hallelujah!" hollers Narciss behind me. "Prayers is answered."

Here she came, Miss Bonnie Dee, sashaying around the table with her little bone razor wide open in her hand. So Uncle Daniel climbed down, good as gold, and sat back in his chair and she got the doodads and commenced to lather his face, like it was any other day. I suppose she always shaved him first thing, and in the dining room!

"*Good* evening," I says.

"Miss Edna Earle," Bonnie Dee turns and remarks to me, "*Court's* opened." There she stood with that razor cocked in her little hand, sending me about my business. "Keep hands down," she pipes to Uncle Daniel, bending down toward him just as bossy, with her little old hip stuck out behind, if you could say she had hips. And when he reached for her, she went around to his other side. I believe she'd missed him.

So I just politely turned on my heel, leaving them both there with fourteen perfect quarts of peach preserves cooling on the back porch behind me. But before I could get down the front steps—

"Miss Edna Earle! Miss Edna Earle!" Narciss came streaking out after me. "Call Dr. Lubanks!"

"I imagine I can handle it," I says. "What is it?"

"It's him," says Bonnie Dee in the door behind her, on one foot.

"Say please, then," I says, and when she did, I went back in. I thought there'd be a little tiny cut on one cheek. But there he stretched. What had happened was, poor Uncle Daniel had gotten out of the habit of knowing what to expect, and when Bonnie Dee came real close to his eye with that razor, biting her tongue as she came, he'd pitched right out of his chair—white as a ghost with lather all over his cheeks and buttermilk dotting his tie.

"Narciss!" I says. "Holler for the closest!"

Grandpa considered he had a perfectly good way of getting in touch with the doctor or anybody else: a Negro on the back of a mule. There's a white man sitting at the crossroads store with a telephone and nothing to do all day but feed those birds.

Dr. Ewbanks had this to say, after he'd come and we'd all finished a good dinner: "Daniel, you know what? You've got to use more judgment around here. You've got a racing heart."

"Sure enough?" says Uncle Daniel. He'd been almost guarded with Dr. Ewbanks ever since Grandpa's funeral. But he smiled clear around the table at that word "heart." "You hear that, Edna Earle?

Hear that, sugar? It's my heart. Promise you won't ever go scootin' off again, then scare me that way coming back."

And Bonnie Dee crosses her heart, but looking around at us all while she does it, like she don't know which one to cross it to, me or Uncle Daniel or Dr. Ewbanks or Narciss or the kitchen cat. Dr. Ewbanks winks at her, and when Uncle Daniel runs around the table, so pale and proud, to get a kiss from her, she says, "Aren't you 'shamed! You always do the wrong thing."

I'll never forgive her.

I had her retroactive allowance right there in my pocketbook—I'd been about to forget it. I replaced my napkin, marched out to the parlor, straight to Grandma's vase on the table. It's two babies pulling a swan and holding something I always thought was a diploma. It had never held anything but calling cards before. I wish you could have seen it the way I left it, stuffed and overflowing with money. You would have wondered what had happened to the parlor table.

And here at the Beulah, coming in singing, Uncle Daniel commenced on, "Oh, my bride has come back to me. Pretty as a picture, and I'm happy beyond compare. Edna Earle got her back for me, you all, and Judge Tip Clanahan sewed it up. It's a court order, everybody. Oh, I remember how I fretted when she tried to run away."

"So do I," I says. "You cried on my shoulder."

"Did I?" he says. "Well, I don't have to cry any more. She's perched out there on the sofa till I get home tonight. I'll hug her and kiss her and I'll give her twenty-five dollars in her little hand. Oh, it would do you good to see her take it."

I put my finger on his lips.

I can't think just what they call that in Court —separate maintenance, I think it is. Only, Uncle Daniel and Bonnie Dee weren't separate as long as he maintained her, is what the difference amounted to. Old Judge Clanahan is pretty well up on things for a man of seventy-five. Uncle Daniel was so happy it was nearly more than he could stand. I sometimes feared for his heart, but he'd forgotten all about that; or she'd made him ashamed of it, once.

He even quit coming to town so much; he'd just send for me to come calling out there if he wanted company. And when I walked in, he'd beam on me and make me look through the bead curtains into the parlor. There she'd be, Bonnie Dee Peacock, curled up on Grandma's rosewood sofa, busy in the light of the lamp—spitting on her finger, turning through the magazines, cutting the coupons out by the stack and weighting them down under the starfish, and eating the kind of fudge *anybody* can make.

And after all I did, lo and behold! Poor Uncle Daniel
—here he came around the Courthouse Square all by
himself one day, in the middle of hot afternoon, carrying both the suitcases and wearing two hats. I was
out in my flowers in front, getting a few weeds out
of the ground with my little old hatchet.

"Edna Earle!" he starts calling as soon as he sees
me. "Have you got a few cold biscuits I could have
before supper, or a little chicken bone I could gnaw
on? Look! I've come."

I jumped up and shook my hatchet at him. "Has
she gone again?" I said. "Now she said she wouldn't
—I heard her."

"Edna Earle, she didn't go a step," says Uncle
Daniel, setting down his suitcases real gentle before

me and taking off both hats. He'd walked all the way in, but made it all in one trip. "She didn't break her promise," he says. "She run me off."

And he walked in and made himself at home right away and didn't take it as hard as you'd imagine. He was so good.

And to tell you the truth, he was happy. This time, he knew where she was. Bonnie Dee was out yonder in the big old lonesome dark house, right in the spot where he most wanted her and where he left her, and where he could think of her being—and here was himself safe with Edna Earle in the Beulah Hotel, where life goes on on all sides. I moved out a lazy drummer and gave Uncle Daniel that big front room upstairs with the Courthouse out the window —the one where he is now. Christmas came, then spring, then Court, and everything in the world was going on, and so many more people were here around than out in the country—than just Bonnie Dee, the Peppers, and the Negroes, the Negroes, the Peppers, and Bonnie Dee. He had a world more to see and talk about here, and he ate like it.

You know, whatever's turned up, we've always *enjoyed* Uncle Daniel so—and he's relied on us to. In fact, he's never hesitated to enjoy himself. But Uncle Daniel never was a bit of good with nothing to talk about. For that, you need a Sistrunk. Something had better happen, for Uncle Daniel to appreciate life. And if he wasn't in the thick of things, and couldn't tell you about them when they did happen, I think he'd just pine and languish. He got that straight from Grandma. Poor Bonnie Dee: I never believed she had one whit of human curiosity. I never, in all the time she was married to Uncle Daniel, heard her say "What next?"

About the time she ran him off is when she began ordering off after everything. The Memphis paper did that. With her name in it that one time, she tried a whole year of it, and here it came, packed with those big, black ads. (Well, her name *was* in again. Mercy on us.)

We heard about the ordering from Narciss, when we saw Narciss in Bonnie Dee's pink voile dress she got married in, parading through Sistrunk's Grocery with a store-bought watermelon wrapped in her arms. Narciss said sure she was dressed up—she spent all her time now saying "Thank you!" As for Miss Bonnie Dee, her new clothes were gorgeous, and she hoped for some of those too some day, when they got holes. Narciss said there were evening dresses and street dresses and hostess dresses and brunch dresses—dresses in boxes and hanging up. Think of something to wear. Bonnie Dee had it.

And *things* began to pour into that house—you'd

think there wouldn't be room. Narciss came chugging into town more times a week than ever, to claim something mighty well wrapped and tied, at the post office or the freight depot, and ride it home on the back seat.

Bonnie Dee even got a washing machine.

"She'll find she's going to need current out there," I says one day. "She may not be prepared for that."

"Yes'm she is," says Narciss. "She prepared. White man back agin yesterday."

"Does she remember it's Grandpa's house she's in?" I says, and Narciss drove off in a fit of the giggles, going zigzag.

But Bonnie Dee kept the washing machine on the front porch, just like any Peacock would be bound to do. Narciss didn't have any idea how to work any machinery but a Studebaker car. I wonder how many of those things they ever did bring under control. I told Narciss I was sure they came with directions hanging on, if there were eyes to read them.

I imagine Bonnie Dee was making hay while the sun shone. Because sure as you're born, if she hadn't run Uncle Daniel off, he'd be there giving things away as quick as she could get them in the door, or up to the porch. She was showing how *she* felt about things. Poor Bonnie Dee, I sometimes do think! Of course down payments were as far as her mind went.

And to crown it all, she got a telephone.

I passed by the place myself, going for a quick ride before dark with Mr. Springer when he was tired (so tired I drove) and Uncle Daniel sitting up behind. Bonnie Dee was out in the yard fully to be seen, in a hunter's green velveteen two-piece dress with a stand-up collar, and Narciss was right behind her in blue, all to watch the man put it in. They waved their hands like crazy at the car going by, and then again going back, blowing dust on all that regalia. Do you think it's ever rung once?

Of course I never asked Uncle Daniel why she ran him off, and don't know to this day. I don't want to know.

So Uncle Daniel was happy in the Beulah and Bonnie Dee was out yonder dressing up and playing lady with Narciss. And it got on toward summer again, but I just couldn't throw myself into it. My conscience pricked me. And pricked me and pricked me. Could I go on letting Uncle Daniel think *that* was the right way to be happy? Could you let your uncle?

I don't know if you can measure love at all. But Lord knows there's a lot of it, and seems to me from all the studying I've done over Uncle Daniel—and he loves more people than you and I put together ever will—that if the main one you've set your heart on isn't speaking for your love, or is out of your reach some way, married or dead, or plain nitwitted, you've still got that love banked up somewhere. What Uncle Daniel did was just bestow his all around quick —men, women, and children. Love! There's always somebody wants it. Uncle Daniel knew that. He's smart in a way you aren't, child.

And that time, he did it talking. In Clay he was right on hand. He took every soul I let in at the Beulah straight to his heart. "Hello, son—what's news?"—then he'd start in. Oh, the stories! He made free with everybody's—he'd tell yours and his and the Man in the Moon's. Not mine: he wouldn't dream I had one, he loves me so—but everybody else's. And things couldn't happen fast enough to suit him. I used to thank my stars this was a Court-house town.

Well, if holding forth is the best way you can keep alive, then *do* it—if you're not outrageously smart to start with and don't have things to do. But *I* was getting *deaf!*

So one Friday morning at nine-thirty when we were sitting down to our cokes in the dining room, I made up my mind to say something. Mr. Springer happened to be here. And Eva Sistrunk had wandered in and sat down—invited herself.

I waited till Uncle Daniel took a swallow—he was giving Mr. Springer's brother-in-law's sister a major operation in Kansas City, Missouri; and thank goodness we never laid eyes on *her*, before her operation or after. Then I said, "Uncle Daniel, listen just a minute—it's a little idea I woke up with. Why don't you try not giving Bonnie Dee the money this Saturday?"

Did I say he'd gone on giving her the money? And that Judge Tip Clanahan and Mr. Bank Sistrunk were both threatening to wash their hands of us for letting her treat us that way.

But I'm a Ponder too. I always got twenty-five dollars in fives from Eloise at the bank, and Uncle Daniel and I climbed in my trusty Ford, every Saturday afternoon after dinner, and ran the money out there. I took it up to the door, folded inside an envelope, and Uncle Daniel sat and watched from the car. Somehow he didn't seem to want to go in, just catch his glimpse. He's a real modest man, you know, and would never push his presence on you unless he thought you wanted him; then he would.

I was perfectly willing about it. I just prissed across the yard and up the steps to the porch and around the washing machine to the front door and called for Narciss. If there'd been a doorbell, I'd have rung it, at my own birthplace. I wore white gloves and a hat, as it was. And Narciss would be waiting to go to town, and holler "Miss Bonnie Dee!" And Bonnie Dee would sashay to the door

wearing some creation and put out her little hand
—not always too shining—and take the envelope.
Uncle Daniel didn't get to see much of her—just
a sleeve.

"Ta ta!"

"You're welcome."

In the car Uncle Daniel raised his hat.

And Narciss caught a ride to town on our running
board.

Once or twice Bonnie Dee had looked out as far
as the road, and waved a little bit, but not too hard.

So now I said to Uncle Daniel—in front of the
others, to hear how it sounded—"Why don't you try
not giving the money to Bonnie Dee? Maybe stop
her charge account at Sistrunk's Store too. Nobody
can live on chicken and ham forever! And see what
transpires. What do you say, Uncle Daniel?"

He says with round eyes, "What would we do on
Saturday?"

"What did you used to do?" I says. "What do
you think of that idea, Mr. Springer?"

Mr. Springer said he thought there was nothing
to lose.

"What do you think, Eva?" I said, because there
she was, fastened to her straw.

"I think just like Mr. Springer, there's nothing
to lose," is all Eva says. Eva can draw you a coat-

of-arms—that's the one thing she can do, or otherwise have to teach school. That's ours, up over the clock: Ponder—with three deer. She says it's not her fault if the gold runs—it's the doorbell ringing or something. She never does *anybody*'s over.

"I think we'll try it, Uncle Daniel," I said. "I made my mind up while the rest of you ate ice."

So I politely kept that Saturday's money for Uncle Daniel, and spoke to the butcher too. And guess what day she sent for us: Monday.

You never saw a happier mortal in your life. He came hopping up those stairs lickety-split to tell me.

I was up there in my room, reading some directions. That's something I find I like to do when I have a few minutes to myself—I don't know about you. How to put on furniture polish, transfer patterns with a hot iron, take off corns, I don't care what it is. I don't have to *do* it. Sometimes I'd rather sit still a minute and read a good quiet set of directions through than any story you'd try to wish off on me.

"Oh, Edna Earle," he says. "What do you think? It worked!"

And all of a sudden I just felt tired. I felt worn out, like when Mr. Springer stays over and makes me go to one of those sad, Monday night movies and never holds my hand at the right places. But I'll tell you what this was: a premonition. Only I couldn't quite place it at the time.

Uncle Daniel was out of breath and spinning his best hat on his finger like a top. "I got the word," he says. "She sent it by three different people—the ice man, the blackberry lady, and the poor blind man with the brooms that liked-to never found me, but *he* told it the best. I was in the barbershop, you know. I just brought the whole string back with me to the hotel and gave them cigars out of the drawer; they all said they smoked. She says to come on. Says to come on before it storms, and this was to you, Edna Earle: please to go by the ice house on the way and put fifty pounds on your bumper for her. Come on, Edna Earle," he says, putting his hat on and putting mine on me. "Come see Bonnie Dee welcome me home. I don't want you to miss it. Where's Mr. Springer? I'd like him to come too."

"Mr. Springer has just bolted out of town," I says. "I heard the car take the corner." Mr. Springer was the perfect listener until he had to go.

"Come without him," says Uncle Daniel, pulling me out of my poor chair. "But make haste. Listen to that! Bonnie Dee was right—she always is—it's fixing to storm." And sure enough, we heard it thunder in the west.

I never thought of the ice again until this day.

Bonnie Dee wouldn't have hesitated asking for the moon! That there should be a smidgen of ice left in Clay at that hour is one of the most unlikely things I ever heard of. What was left of the public cake on the Courthouse steps had run down in a trickle by noon.

Well, to make a long story short, Bonnie Dee sent him word Monday after dinner and was dead as a doornail Monday before supper. Tuesday she was in her grave. Nobody more surprised than the Ponders. It was all I could do to make Uncle Daniel go to *that* funeral.

He did try to give the Peacocks his cemetery lot, but I doubt if he knew what he was doing. They said they bury at Polk, thank you.

He didn't want to go to Polk for anything, no indeed he did not. I had to make him. Then after he got dressed up and all the way down there, he behaved up until the last as well as I did; and it was scorching hot, too. I hope the day they bury me will be a little cooler. But at least people won't have so far to come.

I believe Polk did use to be a town. Mr. Springer told us how to get to it. (He was shooting through Clay headed *east* by Tuesday—there's a great deal of wonder-drug trade going on in all parts of Mississippi.) You start out like you were going to Monterrey, turn at the consolidated school, and bear right till you see a Baptist steeple across a field, and you just leave the gravel and head for that, if you have good tires. And that's Polk. The Peacocks live out from it, but trade there, and, as they said, bury there.

Well, their church is a shell—all burnt out inside. The funeral was further still, at the house.

Portulaca in pie pans was what they set along the front porch. And the mirror on the front of the house: I told you. In the yard not a snap of grass— an old auto tire with verbena growing inside it ninety to nothing, all red. And a tin roof you could just imagine the chinaberries falling on—ping! And now the hot rays of the sun.

The funeral was what you'd expect if you'd ever seen Polk—crowded. It was hot as fluzions in that little front room. A lot of Jacob's-Ladder tops and althea blooms sewed on cardboard crosses, and a salvia wreath with a bee in it. A lot of ferns hauled out of creek bottoms and drooping by the time they got ready for them. People, people, people, flowers, flowers, flowers, and the shades hauled down and the electricity burning itself up, and two preachers both red-headed; but mainly I felt there were Peacocks. Mrs. Peacock was big and fat as a row of pigs, and wore tennis shoes to her daughter's funeral—I guess she couldn't help it. I saw right there at the funeral that Bonnie Dee had been the pick.

We went by in the line, Uncle Daniel tipping on his toes. Such cracks in the floor, and chickens right under your feet! They had the coffin across the hearth on kitchen chairs.

Bonnie Dee was holding a magnolia a little too big for her size. She really did look seventeen. They had her in a Sunday-go-to-meeting dress, old-timey looking and too big for her—never washed or worn, just saved: white. She wouldn't have known herself in it. And a sash so new and blue and shiny it looked like it would break, right out of the Polk general merchandise, tied in a bow around a waist no bigger than your thumb.

When you saw her there, it looked like she could have loved *somebody!*

Uncle Daniel pulled loose from me and circled back. He had Mrs. Peacock by the hand in no time. He said, "Mrs. Peacock, let me tell you something. Your daughter's pretty as a doll."

And Mrs. Peacock says, "Well sir, that's just the way I used to look, but never cared to brag."

They had one big rawboned country preacher on one side of Bonnie Dee, to get up and say look what gold and riches brought you to, and at such an early age—and the other big rawboned country preacher on the other side, to get started praying and not be able to stop. That one asked heavenly mercy for everybody he could think of from the Peacocks on up to the President of the United States. When he got to Uncle Daniel's name I was ready for him and gave Uncle Daniel a good pinch at the right minute. (He generally beams to hear his name called.) My rocking chair was dusty, but at least I got to sit down.

During the service, half the Peacocks—the girls— were still as mice, but the boys, some of them grown men, were all collected out on the porch. Do you know what they did out there, on the other side of the wall from us? Bawled. Howled. Not that they ever did a thing for their sister in life, very likely, or even came to see her, but now they decided to let forth. And do you know all through everything the broom was still standing behind the door in that room?

Once outside, up on the hill, I noticed from the corner of my eye a good many Peacocks buried in the graveyard, well to the top of the hill, where you could look out and see the Clay Courthouse dome like a star in the distance. Right *old* graves, with "Peacock" on them out bold. It may be that the Peacocks at one time used to amount to something (there *are* worthwhile Peacocks, Miss Lutie Powell has vouched for it to Eva Sistrunk), but you'll have a hard time making me believe they're around us. I believe these have always been just about what they are now. Of course, Polk did use to be on the road. But the road left and it didn't get up and follow, and neither did the Peacocks. Up until Bonnie Dee.

It was there at the graveside that Uncle Daniel had his turn. There might have been high foolishness or even trouble—both big red-headed Baptist preachers took hold of him. It was putting her in the ground *he* didn't like.

But I said, very still, "Look, Uncle Daniel. It looks right cool, down yonder in the ground. Here *we* are standing up on top in the burning heat. Let her go."

So he stepped back, for me.

While they were laying on the ferns, away down below us a freight train went by through the empty distance, and the two littlest Peacocks, another generation coming up, stepped forward and waved it out of sight. And I counted the cars—not because I didn't know any better, like them, but because I couldn't help it right then. I counted seventy-nine.

Going back down the hill, Uncle Daniel offered Mrs. Peacock a new pick-up truck for her to haul their watermelons to market; he'd noticed through a slit in the shade, during all that praying, that they were about ripe over the fence, and he complimented the Peacocks on them and said he hoped they'd bring him one. The girls said all right, they would. If he hadn't been so shy with the Peacock boys, he might have given them something; but they didn't get a thing, for the way they acted.

And then, when we got home, they *charged* us.

I know of a case where a man really murdered his wife, with a sure-enough weapon, and her family put on her tombstone, "Vengeance is mine, saith the Lord, I will repay." And his family—the nicer people—had to go take it off with a cold chisel when her family wasn't looking. Ancient history. But thank goodness the Peacocks hadn't heard about that. They just charged us in Court.

Because of course the minute the funeral was over good, and the county paper came out with Eva Sistrunk's write-up and poem, that county attorney we wished on ourselves, Dorris R. Gladney—no friend of the Ponders—out he sailed in a black Ford older than mine, and searched out the Peacocks in Polk and found them, too, and told them what they could do.

They charged Uncle Daniel with murder.

So last week it came up on the docket—it hadn't been anything much of a docket before that, and they shoved a few things out of the way for it.

Old Judge Waite was sitting on the case. Judge Tip Clanahan is not really a judge. What he is is a splendid lawyer and our best friend, even if he is a thousand years old and can't really see where he's going. But lo and behold, Judge Tip told me, just before we got off to the start, he had to let De-Yancey, his grandson, argue Uncle Daniel's case, because he never realized how his strength was leaving him, and he had to go to Hot Springs.

"I was always partial to Daniel, but I'm getting too old for him now," he says. "I got to go to Hot Springs tomorrow."

I knew Grandpa was turning in his grave. "Go out of town?" I says. "You think I'm going to forgive you for it when you get back?"

He gives me a little pinch. The day I don't rate a pinch of some kind from a Clanahan, I'll know I'm past redemption—an old maid.

Uncle Daniel has always considered DeYancey one of his best friends, and was always partial to him until this happened. DeYancey came out and announced that Uncle Daniel wasn't going to open his mouth at his own trial. Not at all, not a word. The trial was going to proceed without him.

It would be like this. I was to testify about what happened. That's very important. Dr. Ewbanks was to testify from the medical point of view. And a few other odds and ends. But Uncle Daniel, the main one, was just supposed to sit there and be good, and not say anything at all. And he felt left out. He didn't understand a bit. It was so unlikely! Why, he loves the limelight.

Everybody in town was indignant with DeYancey when they heard. More than one member of our congregation baked and sent Uncle Daniel his favorite cake—banana—and a Never Fail Devil's Food came from the Clanahans the day Judge Tip went off. Miss Teacake sent a beautiful Prince of Wales cake in black and white stripes—her specialty, but I

couldn't help thinking of *convicts* when I sliced it.
The bank sent a freezer of peach ice cream from
their own peaches, beautifully turned and packed.
Uncle Daniel got the idea things must be more mo-
mentous than he thought. And we couldn't let a soul
get near enough to him for him to do any talking
beforehand—that was the hardest part.

Of course they hadn't done anything *about* Uncle
Daniel: he didn't have to *go* anywhere. They knew
where he was: with me.

"They're letting you roam," says DeYancey to
Uncle Daniel.

"*Roam?*" says he.

"Now that isn't anything for you to worry about,"
says DeYancey. "Just means they can count on you
for coming." As if they could keep him away.

But DeYancey Clanahan was here roaming around
with him. I never saw the like—he was his shadow!
He said, "Come on in the dining room, Daniel, I
want to practice you not talking." That was easier in
the dining room than anywhere else, but it wouldn't
be clear sailing anywhere. Uncle Daniel couldn't bear
to hear out what DeYancey was saying, that was always the trouble.

He managed to keep up his appetite, anyway.
When the day came, he was up with the sun as usual,
and looking pretty cheerful at breakfast. He had on

his new white Sunday suit and white shirt with the baby-blue pinstripe in it, and snow-white shoes and his Sunday tie. He set out when breakfast was over and got a fresh haircut at the barbershop and came back looking fat and fine to me, with a little Else Poulsen rose in his lapel.

Well, the town was jam-packed. Everybody and his brother was on hand, on account of Uncle Daniel's general popularity—and then people not knowing the Ponders but knowing *of* them are just about everywhere you'd look. It was a grand day, hot but with that little breeze blowing that we get from the south.

Uncle Daniel and I didn't get there either early or late, but just on time, and Uncle Daniel had to speak to a world of people—but just "Hello." He was delighted at where our seats were saved—inside the railing. That was the furthest down front he'd ever sat anywhere. I kept my gloves on, and shook open my Japanese fan, and just fanned.

Of course, inside the Courthouse was hot, and one ceiling fan sticks, and the Peacocks coming to town and crowding their way in behind us made the courtroom a good deal hotter.

They came in a body. I didn't count, either time, but I think there were more Peacocks if possible at the trial than at the funeral. I imagine all Polk was there with them; there were people we'd never laid eyes on before in our lives.

The immediate Peacock family had paraded into town in Uncle Daniel's pick-up truck that he'd sent them, as pretty as you please. To see them in Polk was bad enough, but you ought to see them in Clay! Country! And surprised to death at where they found themselves, I bet you a nickel, even if they were the ones started this.

We saw them come in; I turned right around and looked. Old lady Peacock wagged in first, big as a house, in new bedroom slippers this time, with pompons on the toes. She had all of them behind her —girls going down in stairsteps looking funnier and funnier in Bonnie Dee's parceled-out clothes, and boys all ages and sizes and the grown ones with wives and children, and Old Man Peacock bringing up the rear. I didn't remember him at all, but there he was —carrying the lunch. He had a face as red as a Tom turkey and not one tooth to his name, but he had on some new pants. I noticed the tag still poking out the seam when he creaked in at the door.

They're not dying out. Took up the first two rows, with some sitting on laps. And I think it was their dog barked so incessantly at all the dogs in town from the Courthouse porch. Now that the boys weren't hawling, they sat there with their mouths wide open.

The biggest ones' babies just wore their little didies to court, one of them with a brand-new double holster around on top, about to fall off. Couldn't a one of them talk. And of course there was eternal jumping up from the Peacocks to get water. Our drinking fountain in the Courthouse quit working years ago, so it's heaped up with concrete to cover the spout and rounded off and painted blue—our sheriff's wife's idea—and you have to know where to go if you're honestly thirsty.

Uncle Daniel spoke to the Peacocks, but then I saw his face light up, like it only does for a newcomer in his life. And in sailed that lawyer, Dorris R. Gladney. Long, black, buzzardy coat, black suspenders, beaky nose, and on his little finger a diamond bigger than mine, but not half as expensive. Walked too low, and got up and sat down too fast, like all the Gladneys. We all know people who're in a terrible hurry about something! And I understand Mr. Gladney has been peppered with buckshot on several occasions in the course of his career—shows you what kind of people he's thrown with. He rushed up and down the room several times, to show he'd come, and patted the little Peacocks on the head, but they didn't smile an inch.

Then in came DeYancey, real pale, and he patted Uncle Daniel and *he* smiled. And all around us, everybody in the courtroom was talking ninety to nothing when old Judge Waite brought down the gavel and the whole conglomeration sat up.

The other side was first.

Mr. Truex Bodkin came on to start—was led on, rather—he's blind. He's the coroner.

"Heart failure," he said. "Natural causes—I mean *other than* natural causes, could be. That's what I meant—could've been other than natural causes."

"This is the case of the State versus Daniel Ponder we're on today," says the Judge. "Put your mind to your work. Suppose I acted that way." Poor old blind Truex is led back. And do you know who was called next? Nobody you'd ever hear of in a thousand years.

Would you guess, that after all that had been done for him, Uncle Daniel had taken it on himself to send Bonnie Dee *his own message?* That same Saturday I stopped the money, he did it. By word of mouth, of course. And he picked out the slowest, oldest, dirtiest, most brainless old Negro man he could find to send it by. I thought it showed a little ingratitude.

It was Big John—worked for us out there since time was: I don't know what he *did*. Always wore the same hat and shoes and overalls, and couldn't sign his name if life depended. Old man lives off by himself, a way, way back on the place—wonder how far anybody would have to go to find him. *I* never saw where he lived. First, Uncle Daniel had had to send a little Negro from the barbership to get the old one to come in and *learn* the message. Whole thing took all day.

All the money Big John's ever made is right on him now, in his overall pocket, if somebody hasn't taken it again—that's all he wants it for, to carry it around. I expect he's been robbed a hundred times, among the Negroes, but he'll always ask you for money any time he sees you. Of course he and Uncle Daniel get along *fine*. He used to work in the flowers, if you could keep him out of the beds. Dug holes for Grandma; *that's* what she did with Big John.

So here he was. Around his hat is a bunch of full-blown roses, five or six Etoiles in a row, with little short stems stuck down in the hatband—they're still growing in Grandma's garden, in spite of everything.

"Did Mr. Daniel Ponder send word by you to his wife, Miss Bonnie Dee Ponder, on the fourteenth day of June of this year?" is what old Gladney asks him.

Big John agrees with you every time. He nods his head, and the roses bow up and down.

"Now I can tell you're a reliable Negro," says old Gladney. "And I just want you to tell me what the message was. What did Mr. Daniel tell you to say to the lady?"

Big John has a little voice like a whistle the air won't come through just right.

"Go tell Miss Bonnie Dee—go tell Miss Bonnie Dee—" He's getting started.

"Keep on. Tell Miss Bonnie Dee what?"

Big John fixed his mouth, and recited it off. " 'I'm going to kill you dead, Miss Bonnie Dee, if y' don't take m' back.' "

I would have thought Big John would get the message wrong, to begin with—that's one reason I'd never have picked him. But there was no mistaking that—he got *Uncle Daniel's* right!

Old man Gladney says after him, real soft, " 'I'm going to kill you dead, Miss Bonnie Dee—' Did he laugh, I wonder, when he said that?"

DeYancey took objection to that, but Big John didn't even know what laugh was. He just scratched his head up under his hat.

"What made you remember it so good, Uncle?"

Big John still only scratched his head. Finally he says, " 'Cause Mr. Daniel give me a dime."

That was all he could think of. But I knew it was because of that high esteem Big John held Uncle Daniel in, that made him remember so fine. I must say Uncle Daniel held esteem for Big John, too. He always did like him—because of the money he could deposit on him, and then he didn't mind old dirty people the way you and I do. He let Big John come around him and listened to what he said, both. They listened to each other. When you saw them walking white and black together over the back lot, you'd have thought there went two Moguls, looking over the world.

"And what word did Miss Bonnie Dee send back?" says old Gladney. But Big John could remember that about as well as the frizzly hen that comes up to the back door.

"Her didn't have nothing to give me," was the best he could do.

"But Mr. Daniel Ponder did send this message to Miss Bonnie Dee Peacock Ponder, paying you for its safe delivery, Uncle, only two short days before her death: 'I'm going to kill you dead if you don't take me back.' Didn't he?"

"Ain't said to *me*, to *her*," Big John whistled out. "Ain't said to me *that* time. I ain't doin' nothin'. Only but what he tell me."

"That's right. 'I'm going to kill you dead, Miss Bonnie Dee'—and now he's done it," says old Gladney sharp, and no matter how DeYancey's objecting, Big John's agreeing like everything, bobbing his head with those flowers on it under everybody's nose.

DeYancey doesn't want to ask him anything— makes a sign like he's brushing flies away.

"Well, go on, Uncle, I'm through with you," says Gladney.

"He won't go away if you don't give him a nickel,"
I remarks from my seat.

"What for?" says old Gladney, but forks over,
and the old man goes off real pleased. I must say
the whole courtroom smelled of Big John and his
flower garden for a good time afterward.

"I think as a witness, Mr. Gladney, Big John
Beech was worth every bit of that," says DeYancey.

But Uncle Daniel looked to me like his feelings
were already hurt. Big John up there instead of him.

Well, of course I hid it—but *I* was surprised myself at a few who were chosen as witnesses. Here rose
up somebody I'd never expect to see testifying in a
thousand years—Miss Teacake Magee. Old Gladney
begins to tackle her.

"Mrs. Magee, you were married to the defendant,
Mr. Daniel Ponder, for two months in the year 1944,
were you not?"

Miss Teacake had cut bangs, and was putting on
that she could barely whisper; the Judge had to tell
her to speak up so people could hear.

"And divorced?"

You couldn't hear a thing.

"Why were you divorced, may I ask?" says old
Gladney, cheerful-like.

"I just had to let him go," whispers Miss Teacake. That's just what she always says.

"Would you care to describe any features of your

wedded life?" asks old Gladney, and squints like he's taking Miss Teacake's picture there with her mouth open.

"Just a minute," says the Judge. "Miss Edna Earle's girl is standing in the door to find out how many for dinner. I'll ask for a show of hands," and puts up his the first.

It was a table full, I can tell you. Everybody but the Peacocks, it appeared to me. I made a little sign to Ada's sister she'd better kill a few more hens.

Then Gladney gives a long look at the jury and says, "Never mind, Mrs. Magee, we understand perfectly. You'd rather keep it to yourself that you were harboring a booger-man. I won't ask you for another word about it."

Miss Teacake's still looking at him pop-eyed.

Old Gladney backs away on her easy, and De-Yancey hops over and says, "Miss Teacake, just one question will clear this up, for us and you both, I think. In the period of this, your second marriage, did you ever at any time have cause to fear the defendant? Were you scared of Daniel, in other words?"

"Listen here. I don't scare that easy, DeYancey Clanahan," says Miss Teacake in her everyday voice. They tell her just to answer the question. All she says is, "Ever since I lost Professor Magee, I've had to look after myself." She keeps a pistol by her bed, and for all I know, it's loaded.

"But you did ask Mr. Ponder to go. Would anything ever induce you to ask him to come back?" says old Gladney, pointing a finger.

And she hoots out "No!" and scares herself. But by that time they're through with her.

She was mighty dressed up for that five minutes. Had a black silk fan she never did get worked open. Very different from appearing in church, appearing in a court trial. She said afterwards she had no *idea*, when she was asked to testify, that it might be for the other side.

And here next came Narciss—her whole life spent with the Ponders, and now grinning from ear to ear. And she had that little black dog of hers with her. She didn't know any better than let him come, so there he trotted. And her black umbrella she came to town under was folded up and swinging by her skirt.

"Woman, were you working in the Ponder house on the day of which we speak, Monday afternoon the sixteenth of June?" says old Gladney.

"Just let me take off my shades," says Narciss. In town, she wears black glasses with white rims. She folds them in a case that's a celluloid butterfly, from Woolworth's, and says she was there Monday.

He asked her what she was doing the last thing she did for Mrs. Ponder, and when she got around to that answer, she said, "Draggin' old parlor sofa towards the middle of the room like she tole me."

"What for?"

"Sir, lightnin' was fixin to come in de windows. Gittin' out de way."

"Was Mrs. Ponder there in the parlor with you, woman?"

"She ridin' de sofa."

All the Peacocks laughed in court. They didn't mind hearing how lazy they were.

"Was Mrs. Ponder expecting company?"

"That's how come I ironed her apricots dress, all dem little pleats."

"And company came?"

Narciss looked around at me and slapped her leg.

"Who was it? Tell who you saw."

Narciss took him down by telling him she didn't see; but it was us. She ran out of the room first, but she had ears. They let her tell just what she heard, then.

Narciss said, "Hears de car Miss Edna Earle ride around in go umph, comin' to a stop by de tree. Hears Mr. Daniel's voice sound off in a happy-time way, sayin' Miss Bonnie Dee was sure right about de rain. Hears it rainin', lightnin' and thunderin', feets pacin' over de yard. And little dog barkin' at Miss Edna Earle 'cause she didn't bring him a sack of bones."

"So you could say who the company was," says old Gladney, and Narciss says, "Wasn't no spooks." But Judge Waite wouldn't let that count, either question or answer.

"Did Mrs. Ponder herself have a remark to make?" says old Gladney.

"Says, 'Here dey come. Glad to see *anybody*. If it gits anybody, hope it gits dem, not me.'"

Uncle Daniel turned around to me with his face all worked in an O. He always thought whatever Bonnie Dee opened her mouth and said was priceless. He recognized her from *that*.

"Sh!" I said to him.

"Keep on," says old Gladney to Narciss.

"Can't keep on. I's gone by den."

"But you do know this much: at the time you left the parlor, and heard the company coming across the yard and talking, Mrs. Ponder was alive?"

Narciss gave him the most taking-down look she knows. "Alive as you is now."

"And when you saw Mrs. Ponder next?"

"Storm pass over," says Narciss, "I goes in de parlor and asks, 'Did I hear my name?' And dere Mr. Daniel and Miss Edna Earle holding together.

And dere her, stretched out, all dem little pleats to do over, feets pointin' de other way round, and Dr. Lubanks snappin' down her eyes."

"Dead!" hollers Gladney, waving his hand like he had a flag in it. Uncle Daniel raised his eyes and kept watching that flag. "And don't that prove, Narciss, the company had something to do with it? Had everything to do with it! Mr. Daniel Ponder, like Othello of old, Narciss, he entered yonder and went to his lady's couch and he suffocated to death that beautiful, young, innocent, ninety-eight-pound bride of his, out of a fit of pure-D jealousy from the wellsprings of his aging heart."

Narciss's little dog was barking at him and De-Yancey was objecting just as hard, but Narciss plain talks back to him.

"What's that you say, woman?" yells old Gladney, because he was through with her.

"Says naw sir. Don't know *he;* but Mr. *Daniel* didn't do nothin' like dat. His heart ain't grow old neither, by a long shot."

"What do you mean, old woman," yells old Gladney, and comes up and leans over her.

"Means you ain't brought up Mr. Daniel and I has. Find you somebody else," says Narciss.

Gladney says something about that's what the other side had better try to do. He says that's just what he means, there *wasn't* anybody else—since nobody would suspect Miss Edna Earle Ponder of anything —but he stamps away from Narciss like she'd just cheated him fine.

Up jumps DeYancey in his place, and says, "Narciss! At the time you heard company running across the yard, there was a storm breaking loose, was there not?"

"Yes *sir*."

"All right, tell me—what was the reason you only stayed to *hear* the company, not see them? Your best friends on earth! When they came in all wet and wanting to be brushed off, where were you?"

"Ho. I's in de back bedroom under de bed," says Narciss. "Miss Edna Earle's old room."

"Doing what?"

"*Hidin'*. I don't want to get no lightnin' bolts down me. Come lightnin' and thunder, Mr. De-Yancey, you always going to find me clear back under de furthermost part of de bed in de furthermost back room. And ain't comin' out twell it's over."

"The same as ever," says DeYancey, and he smiles. "Now tell me this. What was Miss Bonnie Dee herself generally doing when there was such a thunderstorm?"

"Me and Miss Bonnie Dee, we generally gits down together. Us hides together under Miss Edna Earle's bed when it storms. Another thing we does together, Mr. DeYancey, I occasionally plays jacks with her," says Narciss, "soon as I gits my kitchen swep out."

And at first Bonnie Dee just couldn't stand Negroes! And I like her nerve, where she hid.

"But that Monday," says DeYancey, "that Monday, she didn't get down under anything?"

"She pleadin' company. So us just gits de sofa moved away from de lightnin' best we can. Ugh! I be's all by myself under de bed—listenin' to *dat*." Narciss all at once dies laughing.

"So you can't know what happened right afterward?"

"Sir? I just be's tellin' you what happened," says Narciss. "Boom! Boom! Rackety rack!" Narciss laughs again and the little dog barks with her.

"Narciss! Open your eyes. Both of 'em." And DeYancey gave a whistle. Here came two little Bodkin boys, red as beets, wearing their Scout uniforms and dragging something together down the aisle.

"DeYancey, what is that thing?" asks Judge Waite from the bench.

"Just part of a tree," says DeYancey. He's a modest boy. I don't think it had been cut more than fifteen minutes. "You know what tree that is?" he says to Narciss.

"Know that fig tree other side of Jericho," says Narciss. "It's ours."

"Something specially big and loud *did* happen, Narciss, the minute after you ran under the bed, didn't it?"

DeYancey shakes the tree real soft and says, "Your Honor, I would like to enter as evidence the top four-foot section of the little-blue fig tree the Ponders have always had in their yard, known to all, standing about ten feet away from the chimney of the house, that was struck by a bolt of lightning on Monday afternoon, June the sixteenth, before the defendant and his niece had ever got in the house good. Had they gone in the side door, they would very likely not be with us now. In a moment I'll lay this before Your Honor and the jury. Please to pass it. Look at the lightning marks and the withered leaves, and pass it quietly to your neighbor. I submit that it was the racket this little-blue fig tree made being struck, and the blinding flash of it, just ten short feet from the walls of the Ponder house, that caused the heart of Mrs. Bonnie Dee Peacock Ponder to fail in her bosom. *This* is the racket you heard, Narciss. I told you to open your eyes."

Narciss opened her eyes and shut them again. It was the worst looking old piece of tree you ever saw. It looked like something had skinned down it with claws out. DeYancey switched it back and forth, sh! sh! under Narciss's nose and all at once she opened her mouth but not her eyes and said:

"Storm come closer and closer. Closer and closer, twell a big ball of fire come sidlin' down de air and hit right *yonder*—" she pointed without looking right under DeYancey's feet. "Ugh. You couldn't call it pretty. I feels it clackin' my teeths and twangin' my bones. Nippin' my heels. Den I couldn't no mo' hear and couldn't no mo' see, just smell dem smokes. Ugh. Den far away comes first little sound. It comes louder and louder twell it turn into little black dog whinin' —and pull me out from under de bed." She pointed at the dog without looking and he wagged his tail at her. Then Narciss opens her eyes and laughs, and shouts, "*Yassa! Dat* what git her! *You* hit it!" And all of a sudden she sets her glasses back on and quits her laughing and you can't see a thing more of her but stove black.

All I can say is, that was news to me.

"And *then* you heard the company at the door," says DeYancey, and they just nod at each other.

Old Gladney's right there and says, "Woman, are you prepared to swear on the Holy Scripture here that you know which one came in that house first— those white folks or that ball of fire?"

"*I* ain't got nothin' to do wid it," says Narciss, "which come in first. If white folks and ball of fire both tryin' git in you all's house, you best let *dem* mind who comin' in first. *I* ain't had nothin' to do wid it. *I* under de bed in Miss *Edna Earle's* old room."

She just washed her hands of us. You can't count on them for a single minute. Old Gladney threw his hands in the air, but so did DeYancey.

"Come on, Sport," says Narciss, and she and Sport come on back up the aisle and stand at the back for the rest of it.

So about all old Gladney could do was holler a little—I'll skip over that—and say, "The prosecution rests." That looked like the best they could do, for the time being.

There was a kind of wait while DeYancey rattled his
papers. I never knew what was on those. While he
rattled, he had those little boys haul the fig tree
around the room again, and up the aisle and back
and forth in front of the jury, till Judge Waite made
them quit and brush him off, and then they propped
it up against the wall, in the corner across from the
Confederate battle flag, where I reckon it still may
be, with poor little figs no bigger than buttons still
hanging on it. As Uncle Daniel said, we'll miss those.

The Peacocks were all looking around again. I
don't know what they came expecting. Every once in
a while, old man Peacock had been raising up from
his seat and intoning, "Anybody here got a time-
piece?" And Mrs. Peacock had settled into asking

questions from the people behind her and across the aisle, about Clay—mostly about how many churches we had here and the like. To tell you the truth, Mrs. Peacock talked her way through that trial. If there was one second's wait between things, *she'd* say something. Once she says, "Anybody able to tell me what you can do about all this swelling?" and shows her fingers. "Wake up in the morning all right, and then, along towards now, I look like you'd chopped my fingers all off and stuck 'em back on again." She was right. But she wasn't spending the day in a doctor's waiting room. The Peacock girls sat with their arms tight around each other's necks like a picture-show party—it was hard to tell where one left off and the other began. The littlest brother, about eight, walked up and down with a harmonica in his mouth, breathing through that. The babies kept sliding off laps and streaking for the door, and somebody had to run after them. And of course there was eternal jumping up for water from everybody, and a few water fights— one right in the middle of Miss Teacake's spiel. It was hot, hot, hot. Judge Waite was heard to remark from the bench that this was the hottest weather ever to come within his jurisprudence.

Finally, DeYancey got started and said that what he was undertaking to prove was that the Peacocks didn't have a case on earth. He said it would be very shortly seen that Bonnie Dee was beyond human aid already by the time Uncle Daniel and I put our foot over the sill of the door to that house. I laid my hand on Uncle Daniel's knee. He smiled at me just fine, because here came the blackberry lady, the ice man, and the blind man with the brooms—people he was glad to see again. They fell over each other testifying that Bonnie Dee had sent for Uncle Daniel. They just opened their mouths once and sat down.

Then Dr. Ewbanks. Busy, busy, busy and a widower to boot—everybody has to take him when they can get him. He had an Else Poulsen rose on too.

He told the Court a little white boy called up his house on the telephone from the crossroads store near Ponder Hill that day and told the cook he was wanted out at Mr. Sam's in a hurry, and hung up; and she sent her little boy Elder, who hollered at him, and Dr. Ewbanks was fishing away on Clanahan's Lake, and it was commencing to pour down there too, but he made it on back to shore and back home and out to the Ponders as quick as he could get there in the pouring-down, and found his patient stretched on the sofa there in the parlor with life extinct. He found Uncle Daniel and me needing more attention than she did. He put it down death by misadventure.

When Gladney asks him, he says no, he didn't notice signs of a struggle of any kind; the lady's heart had just up and failed her. It happened sometimes. And if that was how the Ponders had walked in on her and found her, it would never occur to him to doubt a Ponder's word.

Old Gladney scratched his head and pretended to think. "Doc," he says, "what makes the heart fail? What would make a poor young lady's heart fail, without giving warning?"

Dr. Ewbanks waved his hand. "Say fright. Fright due to the electrical storm we had roaming over the countryside at that time," he says. "That's reasonable. Why, a bolt of lightning just narrowly missed *me*, out in my boat on the lake, before I could get it turned around."

Old Gladney edges up and takes a smell of Dr. Ewbanks' rose. He says, "Doctor, how many other cases of the same kind you come across since that storm?"

Dr. Ewbanks says Bonnie Dee was the only case he had, he was glad to say.

"Lightning never strikes twice in the same place, I believe the old saying goes," says Gladney. "Maybe the Ponder family feels like they're all out of danger now, and maybe the Ewbankses do too."

The jury—one or two Ewbankses and Peppers

and a Sistrunk connection or two and a Clanahan by marriage, plus a handful of good old Bodkins—and I wish you'd been here for the selection of the jury! —just looked back at Gladney. He wheels on Dr. Ewbanks with coattails flying. "Would you swear, Dr. Ewbanks, that the death you ascribe to heart failure might not also be ascribed to suffocation?"

"That distinction would be perfectly pointless, Mr. Gladney. Misadventure, Mr. Gladney, in case you'd like to remember this for future occasions," says Dr. Ewbanks, who didn't like anybody to go smelling his rose, "is for all practical purposes an act of God. Like when the baby gets the pillow against its face, and just don't breathe any more." He stands up and smiles. "That answer your question?"

He gave us a nod, and went up the aisle and sat down by Miss Teacake Magee. He'd told me, before the start, he might not be able to stay long enough to see how the case came out; but he did.

And I was next.

I wore this dress—I wear it for everyday, now— and a big Milan hat that's seen me through flood and fire already—but my other glasses, and my dinner ring.

By the time I got settled in the witness chair, De-Yancey had his coat off and his tie undone and his collar open. He's not his grandfather in court, by any

means. And he called me "Ma'am" for the occasion
—I could have killed him.

"Now, ma'am," he says. "The State has been having themselves quite a time over a message Mr.
Daniel Ponder is supposed to have sent his wife just
two days before her death. If we're to rely on the
word of Big John Beech, this message ran, 'I'm going to kill you dead, Miss Bonnie Dee, if you don't
take me back.' Now, ma'am, did you ever hear remarks like that spoken in the Ponder household?"

"Why, certainly," I says. "It was a perfectly nor-
mal household. Threats flew all the time. Yes, sir.
'I'm going to kill you dead—' The rest of it goes,
'if you try that one more time.' "

"Have there been instances in your presence when
Mr. Daniel Ponder said those very words to Miss
Bonnie Dee?"

"Plenty," I says. "And with no results whatever.
Or when she said it to him either."

"Can you tell us right now of one occasion when
Mr. Daniel said it to her?"

"Very probably he said it the first time Bonnie Dee
tried to cut up a leg of his Sunday pants to make herself a skirt out of," I says.

They objected to that—I don't know why. It was
exactly what she made.

"But whatever and whenever the occasion for that

remark, it was a perfectly innocent remark?" says
DeYancey.

"I should hope so."

"So that when Mr. Daniel Ponder sent word to
Miss Bonnie Dee that he was going to kill her if
she didn't take him back, in your estimation it meant
nothing like a real threat?"

"Meant he got it straight from Grandma," I says.
"That's what it means. She said 'I'm going to kill
you' every other breath to him—she raised him.
Gentlest woman on the face of the earth. 'I'll break
your neck,' 'I'll skin you alive,' 'I'll beat your brains
out'—Mercy! How that does bring Grandma back.
Uncle Daniel was brought up like anybody else. And
had a married life like anybody else. I'd hate to hear
the things the *Clanahans* say brought back to my
ears! Mr. Gladney didn't need to traipse over the
fields and find him an old Negro that can't talk good
through his windpipe to tell the Court what word
Uncle Daniel sent his wife—I could have repeated
it without ever hearing it at all, if I'd been asked."

"Thank you, ma'am, I believe you," says De-
Yancey. "And I believe as well as anything in this
world that those words never meant a thing."

After that, I testified in no uncertain terms that
our visit out there that day was Bonnie Dee's idea,
pure and simple.

"Uncle Daniel had been asked to leave in the first place," I says. "Being a gentleman, he would surely wait to be asked to come back before he *went*."

"And you went with Mr. Daniel Ponder for this reunion, ma'am?"

"Would I have missed it for the world?" I said, and looked out at the courtroom. I was certainly on the side of love—that's well known and not worth denying. I said, "How would he have gotten out there otherwise? I drove. Drove us out there at forty, my limit, and pulled up under the pecan tree in the front yard. It was beginning to lightning and thunder at the crossroads; fixing to pour down as we turned in the gate. As I look back—" DeYancey held up his hand, but I went right on and said I had a premonition. You remember it.

"Now tell what you found," says DeYancey, "when you all went in the parlor."

"At first," I says, "I didn't know where I was. Because the furniture was all crazy. And it was so dark. Not any of the lights would turn on, after she had them put in! We tried 'em. Hard to see what she *was* doing. But it lightninged."

"Go on and tell us," he says.

I said, "Well, she *had been* piled up on the parlor sofa in the middle of the room with the windows all down, eating ice out of a tea glass in her best dress. And pushing up candy on the blade of a knife out of a turkey platter she'd poured it out in. I noticed the texture was grainy." I wanted them to see I couldn't hide anything.

"What was she doing now, ma'am?"

"Piled up on the sofa in her best and that's all."

"You mean dead?"

"As a doornail," I says. "I mean what I say, as I always do."

"And how did you know she was dead, ma'am?" asks DeYancey.

I told him it was because I had sense enough to. And I said, "Not a thing would revive her."

"What did you do, ma'am?"

"I hollered. 'Narciss!' I hollered. Because that Negro'd been here in the house since before I was born. 'Narciss!' But she'd gone to cover like a chicken in the daytime when something comes over the sun. 'Narciss!' And not a peep. Not even boo."

Narciss laughed from the back of the courtroom to hear how she did.

"So I ran and reached the spirits of ammonia myself from the top shelf in the bathroom, and ran and held it to her—while you could have counted to a hundred, but it didn't do her a speck of good, as I could have told you beforehand."

"Didn't you try calling any white people?" says DeYancey, trying to hurry me.

"Front and back. I hollered for Otis and Lee Roy

Pepper—they're white; they're responsible for running the place. But they didn't come when I called them—they never do. Turned out they were getting drenched to the skin under a persimmon tree a mile and a half away. So I had to stop a child of ten in his hay wagon, sheltering under a tree, and send him out in it to the crossroads to use the phone at the store and try to find the doctor. *Then* Dr. Ewbanks was out of human cry, till a little nine-year-old colored boy got to him with a bucket on his head. It's a wonder we ever got a doctor to her at all, all of us put together," I says. "No one has ever seen that little white boy or that hay wagon since."

"What was your uncle doing at this time?" asks DeYancey, offhand.

"I quieted him down," I says real calm, so he wouldn't look up. He was looking at the floor. "I told him just to sit there quiet while I listened for her heart. And every time my uncle says, 'Edna Earle, Edna Earle, what do you hear?' I have to say, 'Nothing yet.' 'Then what's that *I* hear?' he says, and I says, 'You must hear your own heart.' "

I heard a real deep sigh come up from everybody, like a breeze. It settled me some. I saw Eva Sistrunk taking out her handkerchief.

"Finally, though, here trotted Dr. Ewbanks in from Clanahan's Lake, in his boots and soaking wet

and a dirty duck hat on his head full of water, track-
ing swamp mud and leaves through the house. He
was surprised to see *me*. He was extremely fishy. I
think he had some baits in a tin can he forgot to
take out. I saw an awful-looking knife sticking out,
and my uncle turns his eyes on it too.

" 'Where's my patient?' says Dr. Ewbanks, and
poor Uncle Daniel falls right over at his feet."

Then I told all about Uncle Daniel stretched out
on the floor and giving him the spirits of ammonia
and how he groaned and how pitiful it was and we
couldn't lift him, and I heard everybody in court
beginning to cry, I believe—but Uncle Daniel was
the loudest. He was looking at me now.

"Well," says DeYancey, "to go back a moment to
the deceased. When you discovered Mrs. Bonnie Dee
Ponder the way she was, ma'am, you were sorry and
upset—but were you greatly surprised?"

"Why, no," I says. "Not greatly surprised. I've
been more surprised in my life by other sudden
deaths in this town."

"Just tell us how long ago you might have been
prepared for something like this."

"She was always out of breath, like somebody
that's been either working or talking as hard as they
could go all day," I says. "For no reason. She
weighed less than a hundred pounds on my scales

in the Beulah lobby—I weighed her. Before she married Uncle Daniel, she fainted in Miss Eva Sistrunk's and my presence in Woolworth's one day, just because the fan went off. Of course, everybody knows Woolworth's would be the most breathless spot in creation to *stay* in."

"So as her niece-in-law, you would testify that Mrs. Bonnie Dee Ponder, to the best of your memory and knowledge, was always frail?"

"A gust of wind might have carried her away, any time." I thought of blowing a kiss out the window to show them, but I felt Uncle Daniel's eyes still on me.

"Your witness," says DeYancey, with a bow to old Gladney.

I looked at Gladney and he looked at me, and drew his hand up to his chin. Grandma Ponder said, "Show me a man wears a diamond ring, and I'll show you a wife beater." There he was.

He says to me, "Mizriz Ponder?" That's what he calls me—Mizriz. He likes to act country, but he don't have all that far to go—he *is* country. "So threats to kill husband or wife never amounts to a hill of beans around here?"

"Depends on who says it," I says, very cool. "It would be different if you take somebody like Williebelle Kilmichael, out in the country. She really empties a load of birdshot into her husband's britches, every so often. Whenever he stands up all through Sunday School, you can be pretty well sure what's happened. Williebelle Kilmichael does it all the time —because she means it. Grandma didn't mean it, Grandpa didn't mean it, I don't mean it—Uncle Daniel don't mean it. You don't mean it."

Just then, too late, I remembered where Mr. Gladney had been peppered, so we heard. He was somebody that knew somebody'd meant it. But I went on fanning, and he went on looking like an old deacon, and opened his mouth and said:

"Well—it may not mean a thing in general, to send a lady a message you're going to kill her if she don't please you, but *what if the day after, she's found dead?*"

"It was two days after. Then everybody's sorry," I says. The Judge makes me change my answer to say it still don't mean anything. "Except love, of course. It's all in a way of speaking," I says. "Putting it into words. With some people, it's little threats. With others, it's liable to be poems."

He says, "All right, Mizriz Ponder, set me straight about something else. I've been worrying about that storm that come up right the same time as your visit—wasn't that too bad for everybody! What worries me most about it is how that ball of fire ever got into you all's house out there. To the best of my memory, every time I ever passed that house, it was covered with lightning rods."

"You're behind the times," I says. "Look up over your head next time you go out of the Courthouse. The first time I had men on the roof after Grandpa Ponder was gone, fixing the holes, I had those things pulled down; Grandma never could stand them. And the Courthouse took them off my hands. Judge Tip Clanahan thought they added enough to the Courthouse to justify the purchase."

"I'm way behind the times," says old Gladney. "Can't keep up with you at all. Now a ball of fire, like that nigger of yours saw, I've got yet to see one—and might not know one if I met it in the road."

"If you don't know what a ball of fire looks like by this time, I'm afraid it's too late to tell you," I says.

He says, "Don't tell me you've seen one, too."

I says, "As a matter of fact, I was the one saw the ball of fire in the Ponder house, the day of the trouble. I saw it the closest-to of anybody."

"Now that'n," he says. "Then you're the very one I ought to ask. Which-a-way did that'n get in, and which-a-way did it get out?"

"You've never been inside our house, Mr. Gladney," I says. "But I'll try to tell you. In down the front chimney. Careened around the parlor a minute, and out through the hall. And if you've never seen a ball of fire go out through bead curtains, it goes as light as a butterfly with wings."

"Do tell!—And what was Mrs. Bonnie Dee Ponder doing," he hollers, "while you was in the parlor *with* her, miratin' at a ball of fire that was supposed to be scarin' her to death? And who else was in there besides? Now the cat's out of the bag!"

Would *you* have known what he was up to? I could have bitten my tongue off! But I didn't show it—I just gave a laugh.

"I beg your pardon, Mr. Gladney," I says. "You aren't a bit straight. The ball of fire you keep going back to was coming out of the parlor when I saw it. That's how I knew where it had been. When Uncle Daniel and I were heading in through the front door of the house, it was heading out the parlor through the curtains—those bead curtains. We practically collided with it in front of the hatrack. I remember I said at the time, 'Whew, Uncle Daniel, did you see that? I bet that scared Bonnie Dee Peacock!' It skirted on down the hall and streaked out the back somewhere to scare the Negroes."

And I sails from the witness stand. I wasn't going to hear another word about balls of fire *that* day.

"Now they've found a witness!" says old Gladney to my back. "A fine witness! A ball of fire! I double-dog dare Mr. Clanahan to produce it after dinner!"

Well, everybody had a good time over that. But when I sat down again by Uncle Daniel, he looked at me like he never saw me before in his life.

"Speaking of dinner," says Judge Waite. "Recess!"—and I could have kissed him, and Ada's sister too, that stood in the door with her finger up.

We had all that company to crowd in at the Beulah dinner table, had to serve it twice, but there was plenty and it was good; and everybody was kind enough to tell me how I did (except Judge Waite, who sat up there by me without opening his mouth except to eat) and made me feel better. I hardly had a chance to swallow my fresh peach pie. When somebody spoke to Uncle Daniel, I tried to answer for him too, if I could. I'm the go-between, that's what I am, between my family and the world. I hardly ever get a word in for myself.

Right across the street were the Peacocks perched on the Courthouse stile, in stairsteps, eating—in the only shade there was. I could tell you what they ate without even seeing it—jelly sandwiches and sweet milk and biscuit and molasses in a tin bucket—poked wells in the biscuit to hold the molasses—and sweet potatoes wrapped in newspaper. That basket was drawing ants all through my testimony, I saw them. The Peacocks finished up with three or four of their own watermelons that couldn't have been any too ripe, to judge by what they left lying on the Courthouse grass for the world to see and pick up.

I certainly was unprepared for what DeYancey Clanahan did after lunch. He asked permission to call up a surprise witness; and he called up one of those blessed Peacocks.

It was one of Bonnie Dee's little old sisters—Johnnie Ree Peacock. The same size and the same hair, and batting her eyes! And there was most of Bonnie Dee's telephone-putting-in costume—very warm for June. And in the most mosquitery little voice you ever heard in your life, with lots of pauses for breath, she testifies that no, she and Bonnie Dee were not twins, they just came real close together, and their mama used to play-like they were twins. You could tell from listening at Johnnie Ree that she didn't have the sense her sister did, though Bonnie Dee never had enough to get alarmed about. Just enough to get married on trial.

Johnnie Ree said Bonnie Dee never did a thing to be ashamed of in her life. And neither did she.

"Even in Memphis?" says DeYancey, prancing around her.

That's what I mean by a tangent. DeYancey didn't

have any business starting to prove that Uncle Daniel *ought* to have got after Bonnie Dee. He just ought to stick to proving that he didn't. He hadn't told me at all, eating that pie, that he was thinking of doing that. If he had, he'd have had another think coming. I didn't want any harm done to Bonnie Dee now! I don't have an ounce of revenge in my body, and neither does Uncle Daniel. The opposite.

"I believe it to be a fact, Miss Peacock, that you once enjoyed a trip to Memphis, Tennessee, with your sister," says DeYancey, and Johnnie Ree's face lights up a smidgen.

She says "Yessir."

I saw it then. Oh, I did well not to make up my mind too hastily about Ovid Springer. I congratulate myself still on that, every night of the world. Mr. Springer would not have hesitated to blacken Uncle Daniel's name before the world by driving sixty-five miles through the hot sun and handing him over a motive on a silver platter. Tired traveling man if you like—but when it came to a murder trial, he'd come running to be in on it. DeYancey had taken time from dinner to catch him on the telephone—he was eating cold cuts in Silver City—and he was headed here, as I found out later, but he had a flat tire in Delhi. I'm afraid that's a good deal like Mr. Springer, from beginning to end. Of course, he never had anybody to look after him.

So Johnnie Ree was just a substitute. But she didn't know it.

DeYancey says, "What kind of time did you have in Memphis?" and she says "Nice," and he says, "Tell us about it."

"Here?" she says.

"Why not?" says DeYancey, smiling that Clanahan smile.

According to Johnnie Ree, in her little mosquito voice, they walked around blocks and blocks and blocks of sidewalks in Memphis without coming to anything but houses, and when they came to stores they rode up and down in stores, and went to movies. Never saw the same show twice. By the second day they started going in the morning and didn't stop all day. Four in one day was their goal. Johnnie Ree wanted to stop and tell us all *Quo Vadis,* as if it had never been to Clay, but DeYancey broke in to ask her where did they stay in Memphis and Johnnie Ree said *she* didn't know: it said "A Home Away from Home." There was a fern a yard broad sitting on the buttress out front that looked like it could eat them up, and that was how she could tell the house from some others that said "A Home Away from Home" too.

And they didn't care to board with the lady, but ate in cafeterias, because you could pick out what you wanted. They had store-bought watermelon in round slices, and store-bought cake that tasted of something queer, like paregoric. Johnnie Ree's voice got a little stronger on the subject of watermelon.

I suppose her tales of Memphis would have gone on the rest of the afternoon (what a blessing that Bonnie Dee didn't *talk* but took after her father!) and everybody was sleepy after dinner anyway, except all of a sudden Uncle Daniel *noticed* her. Noticed Johnnie Ree. (She was on the premises at the funeral, but nothing looked the same then.) I heard his chair scrape. His eyes got real round, and I put my hand on his knee, like I do in church when he begins to sing too fast.

"Why, Bonnie Dee kept something back from me," he says. "Look yonder, Edna Earle. I'm seeing a vision. Why didn't you poke me?"

I says, "Oh, she's got on rags and tags of somebody else's clothes, but she looks like the last of peatime to me." I still hold that Bonnie Dee was the only pretty one they had.

But it was her clothes that Uncle Daniel was seeing.

"Wait till the trial's over, Uncle Daniel," I whispers, and he subsides. He's forgotten the way he looked at me—he's good as gold again.

So Johnnie Ree, who'd talked on and on, and on and on, says, "So we got back home. The end." Like a movie.

"And you behaved like a lady the whole time?" asks DeYancey.

"Yes sir. As far as I know."

"And Bonnie Dee behaved?" cried DeYancey.

"Oh, Bonnie Dee *sure* behaved. She stayed to home."

"What's that?" says DeYancey, stock still. "Who's this sister you've been telling us about? Who did go on this fool's errand, anyway? We were given to understand by a witness now racing toward us to testify, that it was you and your sister Bonnie Dee that were up in Memphis on the loose."

"Bonnie Dee's not the only sister in the world," says Johnnie Ree. "Stand up, Treva."

And up pops a little bitty one. She held her gum still, and turned all the way around, and stood there, till Johnnie Ree says, "Sit down." She was well drilled. Treva had a pin pulling her front together, and guess what the pin was—a little peacock with a colored tail, all kinds of glass stones. I wouldn't be surprised if that wasn't the substance of what she brought back from Memphis.

DeYancey groans. "Mrs. Bonnie Dee Ponder never went herself at all?"

"She was ready to hear what it's like the way we told it. But me and Treva was the ones went, and Bonnie Dee stayed home with Mama," says Johnnie Ree. "She give us two twenties and a five and a ten, and part of her old-lady clothes. So she could get a whole bed to herself and eat Mama's greens."

"But never went?" DeYancey groaned—*everybody* groaned, but the Peacocks.

"She said she was an old, married lady. And it was too late for her to go."

"Why, Mr. Clanahan," says Judge Waite. "I believe you've been wasting our time."

Johnnie Ree brings up her fingers and gives three little scrapes at DeYancey. When she came down, her whole family was just as proud of her as if she'd been valedictorian of the graduating class. The other side didn't want to ask her a thing. She'll remember that trial for the rest of her days.

But mercy. Uncle Daniel was stirring in his chair.

"DeYancey," he says. "You've got a hold of me. Let-a-go."

"Never mind," says DeYancey. "Never you mind."

"I'm fixing to get up there myself." That's what Uncle Daniel said.

"Take the stand? Uh-uh, Daniel. You know what I told you," says DeYancey. "What I told you and told you!"

"Let-a-go your side, Edna Earle," says Uncle Daniel.

"Dear heart," I says.

"It's way past my turn now," says Uncle Daniel. "Let-a-go."

"Edna Earle, he said he wouldn't—didn't you hear him?" says DeYancey across Uncle Daniel's little bow tie.

"You all didn't tell me I was going to have to do so much listening. It ain't good for my constitution," says Uncle Daniel.

I just drew a deep, big sigh. Sometimes I do that, but not like then, in public.

"What's this new commotion? Is this a demand to testify I'm about to hear? I expected it," says the Judge.

I just looked at him.

"That's what it's mounting up to be, Judge," says DeYancey, and he all but wrings his hands then. "Judge, do you have to let him?"

"If he so demands," says Judge Waite. "I've been sitting on the bench a mighty long time, son, since before you were born. I'm here to listen to any and all. Haven't been surprised so far."

"Daniel," DeYancey turns back and says. "If you stand up there, you got to fire me first."

"I'd hate that," says Uncle Daniel, really sorry. "But I'd rather be up there talking myself than hear you and every one of these other folks put together. Turn-a-loose."

"Daniel, it looks to me like now you got to choose between you and me who knows best," DeYancey says.

"I choose me," says Uncle Daniel.

"Don't you think, Daniel, you need to think that over a minute?" says Judge Waite, leaning down like he's finally ashamed of himself.

"Not a bit in the world," says Uncle Daniel.

"Miss Edna Earle's trying her best to say something to you," says Judge Waite.

"I'm going to beat her if she don't stop. And I'm going to *fire him*," says Uncle Daniel. "DeYancey, you're fired."

"Here and now?" says DeYancey, like his heart would break, and Uncle Daniel says, "Sure as you're born. Look—my foot was about to go to sleep." And up he rises.

"Who's going to ask you the questions up there?" says DeYancey, with one last try.

"*Questions!*" says Uncle Daniel. "Who you think I am?"

"Wait, Daniel Ponder," says the Judge. "You've been here enough times and sat through enough sessions of Court to know how it's done as well as I do. You got to let somebody ask you the questions before you can do the talking. I say so."

"Then I choose this gentleman here," says Uncle Daniel—pointing straight at old Gladney, nearly in his open mouth. "I've had my eye on him—he's up and coming. Been at it harder than anybody and I give him a little pat on the back for it. DeYancey's spent most of his time today trying to hold us all down. Run home, DeYancey. Give your grandfather my love."

The judge just made a few signs with his hands, and threw himself back in his chair.

There it came: "Mr. Daniel Ponder!"

Uncle Daniel listened to his name, and just beamed. I wish you could have seen him then, when he walked up there and faced us. He could always show his pleasure so! Round and pink and grand, and beaming out everywhere in his sparkling-white suit. Nobody'd still have a coat on in weather like this—you'd have to be Uncle Daniel, or a candidate.

They let Uncle Daniel hold up his hand and swear, and old Gladney loped over to him, and eyed him, looking up. Uncle Daniel didn't care to sit down. He'd always rather talk standing up.

"Mr. Ponder?"

And Uncle Daniel looked over his shoulder for Grandpa. Nobody had ever called him Mr. Ponder in his life. He was thrilled from the start.

"Mr. Ponder, what is your calling or occupation?" says old Gladney. "Your line of work?"

"Work?" says Uncle Daniel, looking all around, thrilled. "What would I want to work for? I'm rich as Croesus. My father Mr. Sam Ponder left me more than I'd ever know what to do with."

Old Gladney keeps on. "Did you love your wife, Mr. Ponder? I refer to your second wife, Mrs. Bonnie Dee."

"Yes indeed. Oh, I should say I did. You would have loved her too, Mr. Gladney, if you could have had the chance to know her," says poor Uncle Daniel.

"You loved Bonnie Dee," says old Gladney, still keeping on. "You expect the Court to believe that?"

"They've heard it before," Uncle Daniel said, "every one of 'em. She wasn't any bigger than a minute—and pretty as a doll. And a natural-born barber. I'll never find another one like her." But for a second his poor eye wandered.

"And did your wife Bonnie Dee return your love?" asks Gladney.

"Well now, that depended, sir," says poor Uncle Daniel, with the best will in the world. "Edna Earle could have told you all about that. She kept tabs on it." The whole thing might have come out then and there, the whole financial story of the Ponder family. Of course everybody in the room was familiar with it, but nobody wanted to *hear* it.

"On Monday, the sixteenth of June, Mr. Ponder, would you say she loved you?" says old Gladney. "Or loved you not?" He laughed.

They had to recall to Uncle Daniel the day that was—he's the worst person in town on dates and figures—but he said, "Oh, yes indeed, sir. She loved me then."

"Well, Mr. Ponder! If you loved your wife as you declare, and thought there was nobody like her, and your wife—as it depended or not—loved you, and on June the sixteenth she showed she did love you by sending you three proved invitations to return to her side—what did you want to go out there and kill her for?"

Old Gladney shot his old bony finger right in Uncle Daniel's face, surprising him to death. I don't reckon he'd ever really taken it in what the charge was.

Nothing happened in the courtroom except some babies cried.

"Was it because you told her you would? . . . Tell us about it," says old Gladney, real smiley.

They ought never to have let Uncle Daniel up there if they didn't want to hear the story. He smiled back. I tried to hold him with my eye, but it didn't work—not with him up on a stage.

He says, "Do you know, all in all, I've seen mighty little of that girl? First she came, then she went. Then she came, then she run me off. Edna Earle knows, she keeps tabs. Then three kind friends brought word in one day I was welcome. It already looked dark and commenced rumbling towards the west, and we lit out there lickety-split. Now when we got there, I went to hug my wife and kiss her, it had been such a time, Mr. Gladney; but you might hug your wife too hard. Did you ever do that?" asks Uncle Daniel.

Old Gladney says, "No-o-o." People started to laugh at him, then changed their minds and didn't.

"It's a way too easy to do," says Uncle Daniel.

"Sure enough?" says old Gladney, and steps close. "Show me."

Uncle Daniel stood there and hung his head, ashamed of that old fool.

"I'm impervious, I guarantee you," says that old lawyer. "Go ahead, show me what a hug too hard is."

"But that time I didn't," Uncle Daniel tells him. "I went to hug her, but I didn't get to."

"Is that so? How come you didn't get to?" says old Gladney, still close.

That little frown, that I just can't stand to see, came in Uncle Daniel's forehead, and everybody caught their breath but me. I was on my feet.

"Never mind, Uncle Daniel," I calls up. "I've told that."

Judge Waite and old man Gladney and DeYancey Clanahan all three poked their fingers at me, but didn't really notice what I said; nobody noticed. Even Uncle Daniel.

Old Gladney keeps right on. "Listen close to my

next question, Mr. Ponder. I know you can answer it—it ain't hard. When you ran into the parlor to hug her—only you didn't get to—did Bonnie Dee speak to you?"

DeYancey was leaping up and snapping his fingers, objecting his heart out, but what good does objecting to Uncle Daniel do? You just get fired. Uncle Daniel would have fired the angel Gabriel, right that minute, for the same thing. You never could stop Uncle Daniel from going on, once you let him know he had your ears. And now everybody was galvanized.

"Hollered! She hollered at me. 'I don't appreciate lightning and thunder a bit!' " said Uncle Daniel —proudly. And in her voice. He did have it down to a T, like he could always do bird calls. He looked over our heads for Narciss, and smiled at her.

Everybody let out one of those big courtroom sighs.

"She spoke. She hollered. She was alive and strong," says Gladney. "And what did *you* say, sir?"

Uncle Daniel changed. He got carnation-color. He looked down at the Stetson between his fingers and all that time went by while he turned it round and then sighted through the ventilation holes he'd cut in the crown. Then he said quick, "I said 'Catch her, Edna Earle!' "

Gladney says, "Bonnie Dee was running?"

"No, falling," says Uncle Daniel. "Falling to the floor."

"And did Miss Edna Earle catch her?"

"No, sir," says Uncle Daniel. "She can't catch."

I could have died right there.

"And what had you done to her first?" whispers old Gladney.

Uncle Daniel whispers back, "Nothing."

"You laid hands on her first!" yells Gladney.

"On Bonnie Dee? No, you can hug your wife too hard," says Uncle Daniel, "when you haven't seen her in a long time. But I didn't get to. Dr. Ewbanks had to raise me up and tend to me. I'm more poorly than I look."

"I congratulate you just the same," says Gladney, straightening up. "You got a reliable memory. You set us going on the right track. You got the most reliable memory in Court. We'll see who can remember the rest of it now. Much obliged—Mr. Ponder."

"Daniel!" says DeYancey, pushing in front of Gladney and pulling Uncle Daniel by the sleeve. "I know you fired me, but we've got to disregard it —everything! Listen to me: were you ever in the asylum?"

"Look, Tadpole," Uncle Daniel says—he still calls DeYancey that from the time they played so nicely together, "if there's anybody knows the answer to that already, it's you and your granddaddy. Your granddaddy got me in, him and somebody else." Till that good day, Uncle Daniel had never mentioned Grandpa's name from the time he died.

"Thanks, boy," says DeYancey, and to Gladney he says, "That's the witness. I ask that his evidence be stricken—"

Old Gladney was already wheeling back in his coattails. "Mr. Ponder! Were you *discharged* from the asylum?"

"Why, sure," says Uncle Daniel. "Look where I am. Man alive, if Judge Clanahan could get me in, he could get me out. Couldn't he, Tadpole? Where is he, by the way—I've missed his face. Give him my love."

"Thank you, Mr. Ponder—*I* thank you. That'll be all. I'd now be very happy to cross-examine Miss Edna Earle Ponder once more, if she don't mind," old Gladney says.

But Uncle Daniel says, "Wait. You want the story, don't you? There's a world more to it than that. I can beat Edna Earle the world and all telling it. I'll start over for you."

And I knew he did want to tell it—I was the one knew that better than anybody. But I leaped up one more time where I was.

"Never mind, Uncle Daniel! Listen to Edna Earle," I says. "If you tell that, nobody'll ever be able to believe you again—not another word you say. You hear me?"

He needn't think I was going to let him tell it now. After guarding him heart and soul a whole week —a whole lifetime! How he came into the parlor all beaming pleasure and went shining up to her to kiss her and she just jumped away when the storm went boom. Like he brought it. And after she'd gone to the trouble to send for him, and we'd gone to the trouble to come, she just looked at him with her little coon eyes, and would have sent him back if I hadn't been there. She never said good evening to me. When I spoke she held her ears. So I sat myself down on the piano stool, crossed my knees, and waited for the visit to start.

Uncle Daniel sat down beside her and she wouldn't even look. She pulled herself in a little knot at the other end of the sofa. Here came a flash of lightning bigger than the rest, and thunder on top of it, and she buried her face in the pillow and started to cry. So the tassel of Grandma's antimacassar came off in Uncle Daniel's hand and he reached out and tickled her with it, on the ankle.

The storm got closer and he tickled a little more. He made the little tassel travel up to her knee. He wouldn't call it touching her—it was tickling her; though she didn't want one any more right now than the other.

Of course, Uncle Daniel and I had both been brought up to be mortally afraid of electricity ourselves. I'd overcome it, by sheer force of character —but I didn't know Uncle Daniel had. I believe he overcame it then. I believe for Bonnie Dee's sake he shut his own ears and eyes to it and just gave himself up to trying to make her stop crying.

And all the while it was more like a furnace in there, and noisy and bright as Kingdom Come. Grandpa Ponder's house shook! And Bonnie Dee rammed harder into the pillow and shrieked and put out her hands behind her, but that didn't do any good. When the storm got right over the house, he went right to the top with "creep-mousie," up between those bony little shoulder blades to the nape of her neck and her ear—with the sweetest, most forbearing smile on his face, a forgetful smile. Like he forgot everything then that she ever did to him, how changeable she'd been.

But you can't make a real tickler stop unless you play dead. The youngest of all knows that.

And that's what I thought she did. Her hands fluttered and stopped, then her whole little length slipped out from under his fingers, and rolled down

to the floor, just as easy as nod, and stayed there—
with her dress up to her knees and her hair down
over her face. I thought she'd done it on purpose.

"Well!" I says to Uncle Daniel. "I don't think
it's such a treat to get sent after. The first thing
Bonnie Dee does when we get here is far from ladylike." I thought that would make her sit up.

"Catch her, Edna Earle," he says. "Catch her."
That's when he said it.

I marched over and pulled up her hand, and it
hung a weight in mine like her ball and jacks were
in it. So did her other hand when I pulled it. I said
"Bonnie Dee Peacock."

That's when the ball of fire came down the chimney and charged around the room. (The ball of fire
Narciss took for her story.) That didn't scare me. I
didn't like it, but it didn't scare me: it was about as
big as your head. It went up the curtains and out
through them into the hall like a butterfly. I was
waiting for Bonnie Dee to answer to her name.

When she wouldn't do it, I spread back that baby
hair to see what was the matter. She was dead as a
doornail. And she'd died laughing.

I could have shaken her for it. She'd never laughed
for Uncle Daniel before in her life. And even if she
had, that's not the same thing as smiling; you may
think it is, but I don't.

I was in a quandary what to do. I had hold of her, and nobody ought to stay on the floor. It was still carrying on everywhere you looked. I hauled her back up on the sofa the best I could. She was trouble—little as she was, she was a whole heap heavier than she looked. And her dress was all over the place—those peach-colored pleats blinking on and off in the lightning, and like everything else you touched, as warm as dinner plates.

Poor Uncle Daniel had never stirred an inch since she went out of his reach, except to draw up his feet. Now, after where I put her back, and let her be, he hitched both arms around his knees and stayed that way.

Of course I couldn't go off and leave him there, to get help. I only ran after the ammonia, and that only takes a second, because I know where to find it. In the bathroom I glanced in the mirror, to see how I was taking it, and got the fright of my life. Edna Earle, I said, you look old as the hills! It was a different mirror, was the secret—it magnified my face by a thousand times—something Bonnie Dee had sent off for and it had come. I ran back, but the laugh didn't go away—for all I went out of the room a minute, and for all Uncle Daniel sat still as a mouse, and for all the spirits of ammonia I offered her or the drenching I gave her face. That ice in her glass was all water now.

I never thought of the telephone! I got the boy on the hay wagon by the simple expedient of opening the window and hollering as loud as I could, till it brought him. In came Dr. Ewbanks, finally, in his boots, and pushed that yellow fluff back just the way I did.

"You don't mean she's flew the coop?" he says.

And Uncle Daniel didn't wait. He tumbled head-long to the doctor's feet, and didn't know any more about *that*. Thank the Lord for small favors.

Well, I could have told the courtroom that as well as Uncle Daniel, and carried it on a little further. But I had too much sense to even try. I never lied in my life before, that I know of, by either saying or holding back, but I flatter myself that when the time came, I was equal to cither one. I was only thankful I didn't have to explain it to Grandpa.

Maybe what's hard to believe about the truth is who it happens to. Everybody knows Uncle Daniel Ponder—he wouldn't have done anything to any-body in the world for all you could give him, and nobody, you'd think, would do anything to him. Why, he's been brought up in a world of love.

So I stopped the words on his lips, from where I stood. "You can't tell it, Uncle Daniel," I says firm. "Nobody'll believe it."

"You can tell *me*, Mr. Ponder," says old Gladney. "Remember, you picked me out. I'll believe it, easy as pie. What had you gone and done to that precious girl?"

"That's enough, Uncle Daniel," I says, real firm and real loud. "You can't answer that. You can't tell it to a soul."

And Uncle Daniel's mouth opens—and sure enough, he can't.

Uncle Daniel stood still a minute on the witness stand. Then he flung both arms wide, and his coat flew open. And there were all his pockets lined and bursting with money. I told you he looked fat. He stepped down to the floor, and out through the railing, and starts up the aisle, and commences handing out big green handfuls as he comes, on both sides. Eloise Clanahan climbed over her new beau and scooted out of the courtroom like the Devil was after her.

"What is this-here?" says Gladney. Poor man, he was taken by surprise. He ran and caught onto Uncle Daniel's coattails. "Come back, man, the trial's not over!"

That's all *he* knew.

"What is this?" says DeYancey. "Edna Earle, what have you brought on?"

And "Order!" says the Judge.

Uncle Daniel doesn't say anything, but reaches in with both hands. He brings out more money than you could shake a stick at. He made every row, like he was taking up collection in church, but doing the very opposite. He reached in and reached in, handed out and handed out. He was getting rid of it all right there in Court, as fast and businesslike as he could.

Everybody in town, Ewbankses, Magees, Sistrunks, old Miss Ouida Sampson that hadn't been out of her house in years but wanted to be carried to this, and couldn't hear a word that was said, but put out her little skin-and-bones hand now for what came her way; and all the children in town (they were loose) and total strangers who'll always go to anything, and the coroner, that blind Bodkin, everybody that could walk and two that couldn't, got some.

Some put their hands out like they were almost scared not to. The Peacocks' hung back the longest, with their mouths open, but the little ones in diapers soon began to strike out and run after floating bills that got loose and were flying around. And old Gladney sends up a cry to the Peacocks then, "Grab what you can get!"

There was Bedlam. And passing the window Uncle Daniel let fly some bills that they never found, and I reckon the dogs chewed them up. Uncle Daniel was only trying to give away all he had, that's all. Everything to his name.

Old Mr. Jeff Ewbanks—he's Dr. Ewbanks' father and the mayor, frail, frail—he says, "Stop him, Miss Edna Earle! Stop him, young lady!"

Now I'll tell you something: anything Uncle Daniel has left after some future day is supposed to be mine. I'm the inheritor. I'm the last one, isn't that a scream? The last Ponder. But with one fling of the hand I showed the mayor *my* stand: I'd never stop Uncle Daniel for the world. This was his day, and anyway, you couldn't any more stop Uncle Daniel from giving away than you could stop a bird from flying.

Of course the *lawyers* couldn't do anything; De-Yancey was fired, to boot. And Judge Waite wasn't even born in this county. Finally, it was too much for guess who?

It was Miss Lutie Powell who spoke up *directly* to Uncle Daniel. She was his old teacher, that's who *she* was. Afraid of no man. She points her palmetto at him and says, "Go back to your seat this minute, Daniel Ponder. Do you know how much money you've thrown away in the last five minutes? Have you any idea of how much you've got left? What do you say to me, Daniel?"

It froze Uncle Daniel for about one half minute. Then he just skipped Miss Lutie and went on.

Next, Mr. Bank Sistrunk stands up and roars out, "Daniel Ponder! Where did you *get* that money?"

It was too late then.

"Well," says Miss Missionary Sistrunk—the old-

est one, returned from wildest Africa just twenty-
four hours before—"the Ponders as I've always been
told did not burn their cotton when Sherman came,
and maybe this is their judgment."

"Take that back, Miss Florette," I says over people's heads. "The Ponders did not make their money
that way. You got yours suing," I says. "What if
that train hadn't hit Professor Magee, where'd any
Sistrunks be today? Ours was pine trees and 'way
after Sherman, and you know it."

" 'Twas the same Yankees you sold it to!" That
was Mr. Sistrunk. Why, he was beside himself. But
Uncle Daniel just then got to him and gave him a
single hundred-dollar bill, and shuts him up. You
know, I think people have lost the power to be
ashamed of themselves.

After all, it was our bank—Mr. Sistrunk just ran
it. It turned out later that Uncle Daniel had gone
to the bank early that morning—he was roaming—
right after his haircut, and nobody was there yet but
Eloise. So Uncle Daniel just took the opportunity of
asking for it all: he asked Eloise for it and Eloise
just gave it to him. She said she did it to cheer him
up. It took every bit the bank had that day, and then
they owed him some. They still do. The bank had
never, never, never let Uncle Daniel get his hands
on cash. It's just a rule of Clay. Mr. Bank Sistrunk

says he's going to have to let Eloise Clanahan go.

And you know—she was right. It *was* cheering him up. There on Uncle Daniel's face had come back the ghost of a smile. By that time, I think that all he wanted was our approval.

(And I don't give a whoop for your approval! You don't think I betrayed him by not letting him betray himself, do you?)

Most people were on their feet in Court by then, and some crying—old ladies that remembered Grandma—and Judge Waite just sits there, leaning his head on his hand. Then leans it on the other hand. Then stands up and raises both arms, without words. That's the way DeYancey behaved too, but more like a jack-in-the-box, being younger. I just sat there and took note.

I don't think any of those people that day would have ever accepted it from Uncle Daniel—money! —if they'd known what else to do. Not to know how to take what's offered shows your manners— but there's a dividing line somewhere. Of course they could have taken it and then given it back to *me*, later. Nobody ever seemed to think of that solution, except Edna Earle Ponder. Surely they're not beginning to be scared of *me*.

And Uncle Daniel had got right back to where he started from. He went from giving away to falling

in love, and from falling in love to talking, and from
talking to losing what he had, and from losing what
he had to being run off, and from being run off
straight back to giving away again.

Only it was worse than before, and more public.
The worst thing you can give away is money—I
learned that, if Uncle Daniel didn't. You and them
are both done for then, somehow; you can't go on
after it, and still be you and them. Don't ever give
me a million dollars! It'll come between us.

I wish you could have seen Miss Teacake Magee
when she saw Uncle Daniel coming. She let out two
little hoots, like a train going round the bend, and
fell over with her cheek on Dr. Ewbanks' shoulder.
Uncle Daniel put a little money in her lap anyway,
and gave her knee a stir.

The Judge charged the jury somewhere along there,
but I don't remember a bit of what he said, and
doubt if he does either, and they just went around
the door and came right back, hating to miss anything
in the courtroom. Uncle Daniel heard the commotion
of them coming in and worked back that way and
let fly a great big handful over their heads.

And all the children were jumping up and down
and running around Uncle Daniel for dear life and
calling him, and he threw them the change out of

his pants pockets, like he always did. He didn't re-alize they grew up right there and wanted some big money now.

The Baptist preacher—Brother Barfield, always on hand—rose up and made his voice heard over the storm. (Our preacher was home praying for us, where he belonged.) He said he thought all the money here unclaimed by Mr. Daniel Ponder (*that* was a funny way to put it) should be turned over to the Baptist Church, which needed it. But old lady Peacock—and such a Baptist, you remember *two* preachers at the funeral—hollers back gay as a lark, "Finders keepers!" and showed him her hands full.

"Si-lence!" says Judge Waite. He's famous for that cry. That may be why they got him for this trial. But he was shaking both fists, too. I don't know that I ever saw him that wild before. "Let the pub-lic please to remember where they are at. I have never, in all my jurisprudence, seen more disrespect-ful behavior and greater commotion and goings-on at a trial. Put that right in the record, Birdie Nell. This jury, *mirabile dictu*, has reached a verdict. Now you *hear* it."

So the jury said Not Guilty. It almost got lost in the rush. Anyway, that old Gladney cringed. I hoped he was done for, but I expect he's not—he's probably going straight ahead from here and will end up Governor of Mississippi. Nobody showed a sign of going home.

Uncle Daniel saw that, and patted all over his pockets and threw the children what you could see was the last few pennies he could find. When it was all gone, he just went through the motions—like scattering chickenfeed.

"Edna Earle," he calls to me at last, "you got any money?"

"No, Uncle Daniel," I calls back, "I haven't got any money."

"Well, mine's all vamoosed," he says, and just stops. He spreads his hands. Eva Sistrunk had the nerve to tell me later that everybody felt so bad about Uncle Daniel at that moment that if he hadn't been so prominent and who he was, they would have taken up a collection for him. Like he was anybody else just acquitted of murder!

So that was about all.

There's no telling how much the Peacocks got—but remember how many there are, and how many hands that made. I'm sure I saw one of the babies eating money. Furthermore, before they left, the Peacocks had claimed kin with poor old Miss Ouida Sampson, but I don't believe she knew a thing about it. She just nods her head that way—whatever happens.

Well! I'd hate to have to go through it all again.

Outside, everybody was running ahead down the Courthouse steps—ahead of Uncle Daniel and me. We came down together. I heard the Judge's wife blowing the horn for him, but he was going down real heavy and slow and leaning on DeYancey Clanahan, and then I saw DeYancey hurrying off to get drunk. That's the Clanahan failing. Old Gladney came last of all, and all alone, and jumped in his Ford and hit the highway.

There was a little crowd held up at the stile, and a minute when we caught up with the Peacocks. Uncle Daniel pulled at the corner of Johnnie Ree's dress as she was going over the top and asked if he could come take her riding one of these days.

But she says, "No thank you!" It's all gone to her head as quick as that.

For a minute he just stood still in the bright sun, like the cake of ice that was melting there that day.

"Come with me, Uncle Daniel," I says, and put my arm through his.

Uncle Daniel comes on with me, real quiet, over the stile to the street full of cars getting started and going home. We go fronting through the children still clinging around, that don't understand there's not any more left.

And here came Mr. Springer, for the Lord's sake,

chugging around the corner. Uncle Daniel didn't even see him. We crossed the street while Mr. Springer had to hold the brakes for us. I didn't give a good continental.

Oh, for a minute in the street there, I wished that Uncle Daniel had just whipped out and taken a stick to Bonnie Dee—out of good hard temper! Of course never meaning to kill her. And there *is* temper, on Grandpa's side. Uncle Daniel was just born without it. He might have picked up Grandpa's trusty old stick hanging right there on the hatrack where Grandpa left it, and whacked her one when she wasn't glad to see him. That would have gone down a whole lot easier in Clay. Even with the Peacocks, who didn't know anything was out of the way till a man like Gladney spotted it right through a poem and had to haul off and tell them about it. Sometimes I think old Gladney dreamed the whole thing up himself, for lack of something to do, out of his evil mind.

Well, if he did, the verdict served him right.

"Edna Earle," says Uncle Daniel, when I got him safe through the street and the front door of this hotel, "I've got good news for you. I'm coming to live with you for keeps. In the best room you can give me in the Beulah Hotel."

I says, "Grand." I says, "That's the room you're

in already, Number One at the head of the stairs."

He hung his hat there and went right on through the lobby and started up that staircase without looking around for a soul—and there really wasn't a soul. I stood there at the foot and watched him go. I started to call to him I'd give him the hotel back. But I thought the next minute: no use starting him off again.

He got as far as the landing and turned around and called down, "You fooled me up yonder at Court this afternoon, Edna Earle, I declare you did. But never mind—I'm staying just the same. You didn't fool me as bad as Bonnie Dee did."

"Well, I hope not," I said. "You better go on up and wash your face and hands, and lie down till you're ready for your supper. Just let me call you."

But he don't enjoy it any more. Empty house, empty hotel, might as well be an empty town. He don't know what's become of everybody. Even the preacher says he has a catch in his back, just temporary. And if people are going to try being ashamed of Uncle Daniel, he's going to feel it. *I'm* here, and just the same as I always was and will be, but then he never was afraid of losing me.

So Grandpa's house is standing out there in grass. The Peppers are keeping on with the crop, though they don't have a notion who for, or where they stand. Who does?

You see, that money has come between the Ponders and everybody else in town. There it still is, on their hands. (I'm sure the Peacocks have spent theirs in Polk, without a qualm—for something they don't have the ghost of a use for.) Here Clay sits and don't know what to do with it. All dressed up and no place to go, so to speak. There's been talk, I hear, of something civic—an arch to straddle the highway with the words in lights, "Clay. If You Lived Here You'd Be Home Now." I spot that as a Sistrunk idea.

And I haven't seen a soul in here in three days. You'd think Eva Sistrunk, at least, would be beginning to get lonesome. So I wasn't sorry to see you come in. Uncle Daniel will express a welcome too. You're the first!

He comes down a little later every night. One of these times I'm going to start him on a good course of calomel-and-quinine. I'm a pretty good doser myself. But it's time now supper was ready.

Narciss! Put three on the table!

At least I've got somebody now that can cook— if she just would. But Narciss don't cook good any more. I hate to tell you—her rice won't stand apart. She don't cook any better than Ada or Ada's sister ever did. She claims she's lonesome in town.

And you know, Bonnie Dee Peacock, ordinary as she was and trial as she was to put up with—she's the kind of person you do miss. I don't know why —deliver me from giving you the *reason*. You could look and find her like anywhere. Though I'm sure Bonnie Dee and Uncle Daniel were as happy together as most married people.

And it may be anybody's heart would quail, trying to keep up with Uncle Daniel's. But I don't give Bonnie Dee Peacock too much credit for trying.

I'm going to holler—*Uncle Daniel!*

I'd like to warn you again, he may try to give you something—may think he's got something to give. If he does, do me a favor. Make out like you accept it. Tell him thank you.

Uncle Daniel? Uncle Daniel! We've got company!

Now he'll be down.

*Books by Eudora Welty
available in paperback editions
from Harcourt Brace Jovanovich, Publishers*